PRAISE FOR VIVIAN AREND

"Once again, Vivian Arend proves that she knows her readers well and is able to give us the pieces of happiness that allows us to hold on to our patience until the next release."
– *Romance Witch Reviews*

"With sassy, spirited and familiar characters, Vivian Arend invites the readers to bear witness to the love and commitment of the characters we love."
~ *The Reading Cafe*

"Brilliant, raw, imaginative, irresistible!!"
~ *Avon Romance*

"The Heart Falls series is such a funny and sexy contemporary series, and I highly recommend to fans of contemporary romance."
~ *Blogging by Liza*

"Arend became a favorite author of mine because not only does she write about sexy cowboys, she gives us families who love and take care of each other."
~ *SmexyBooks*

"This was my first Vivian Arend story, and I know I want more!"
~ *Red Hot Plus Blue Reads*

ALSO BY VIVIAN AREND

Heart Falls Vignette & Novella Collection
Three Weddings and a Baby
Girls' Night Out
Rose's One Night to Forever
Fern's Date with Destiny
Hot Times in Heart Falls

The Stones of Heart Falls
A Rancher's Heart
A Rancher's Song
A Rancher's Bride
A Rancher's Love
A Rancher's Vow

The Colemans of Heart Falls
The Cowgirl's Forever Love
The Cowgirl's Secret Love
The Cowgirl's Chosen Love

A full list of Vivian's print titles is available on her website:
www.vivianarend.com

HOT TIMES IN HEART FALLS

HEART FALLS VIGNETTES & NOVELLAS
COLLECTION
BOOK 5

VIVIAN AREND

Hot Times in Heart Falls
Copyright © 2026 by Arend Publishing Inc.
Digital ISBN: 978-1-998508-55-6
Print ISBN: 978-1-998508-63-1
Edited by Angie Ramey
Cover Design © Damonza
Proofed by Linda Levy

MESSAGE FROM VIVIAN

Here we go again!

For one final time, we're gathered up the tidbits and flashes of life beyond the happily-ever-after for our Heart Falls friends. Or...*almost* final.

As always, these slice of life moments were written specifically for you, the reader has already enjoyed the main stories. This time, some of these visits with favourite friends are on the hotter side. Life carries on with that part of the story, as well.

You've seen a couple of these already, or a part of them, at Christmas time, or ahead of a new release.

This collection also contains three brand new stories for you!

I have to admit that one of these stories has been taking up space in my brain for far too long. Yes, I finally get to share the story of when Ginny and Tucker became a secret couple. I can't wait to share that with you, as well as a story for a more recent couple to appear in the books, Edison (nurse at the Heart Falls clinic) and Kevin (from High Water).

And finally a holiday visit with all the people associated with the firehall!

Check the intros first to see where the individual stories fit into the full series reading order if you want to avoid spoilers for books you haven't yet read!

There's also a reading order on the next page if you want to make sure you've read all the books so far. I've jumped around a little between series, so if you've missed any, now's the time to catch up!

I hope these stories make you smile.

With love from me and your friends in Heart Falls.

Viv

HEART FALLS SERIES

If you would like to read all the Heart Falls books in Chronological reading order:

A Rancher's Heart (The Stones of Heart Falls, Book 1)

Surprised at Bootstomp Point (Heart Falls Vignette Collection Vol. 1)

A Rancher's Song (The Stones of Heart Falls, Book 2)

A Firefighter's Christmas Gift (Holidays in Heart Falls, Book 1)

A Rancher's Bride (The Stones of Heart Falls, Book 3)

Heartfelt at Heart Falls (Heart Falls Vignette Collection Vol. 1)

The Cowgirl's Forever Love (The Colemans of Heart Falls, Book 1)

A Wild Horse Wedding (Heart Falls Vignette Collection Vol. 1)

The Cowgirl's Secret Love (The Colemans of Heart Falls, Book 2)

The Cowgirl's Chosen Love (The Colemans of Heart Falls, Book 3)

Glamour & Truth (Heart Falls Vignette & Novella Collection: Vol. 2)

A Soldier's Christmas Wish (Holidays in Heart Falls, Book 2)

Oh, Baby! (Heart Falls Vignette Collection Vol. 1)

A Hero's Christmas Hope (Holidays in Heart Falls, Book 3)

Ashton's Birthday Surprise (Heart Falls Vignette & Novella Collection: Vol. 2)

*this story is actually the first chronologically in the Heart Falls world but won't make sense if you start with it. We recommend reading it after A Rancher's Love.

HEART FALLS FAMILY TREE

Heart Falls
during **Hot Times in Heart Falls** *Vignette*
Collection

Heart Falls Firehall

Brad Ford and Hanna Lane
crissy, drew, ethan
3. A Firefighter's Christmas Gift

Mack Klassen & Brooke Silver
landon, expecting
8. A Soldier's Christmas Wish

Ryan Zhao & Madison Joy
talia, justin, mikayla
10. A Hero's Christmas Hope

Alex Thorne & Yvette Wright
12. A Cowboy's Christmas List

Ashton Stewart & Sonora Fallen
13. A Rancher's Christmas Kiss

The Fields Family

malachi & sophie

Ivy & Walker
Carter, Chloe, Harper
2. A Rancher's Song
14. A Forever Family (Vignettes Vol 2)

Rose & Chance
15. Rose's One Night to Forever

Fern & Cody
19. Fern's Date with Destiny

The Stone Family

walter(d) & deb(d)

Caleb & Tamara
sasha, emma, tyler
1. A Rancher's Heart

Luke & Kelli
kyle, expecting
4. A Rancher's Bride

Ginny & Tucker Stewart
demi, expecting
11. A Rancher's Love

Dustin & Charity
16. A Rancher's Vow

Whiskey Creek Colemans

george & sally (d)

Karen & Finn Marlette
scott
6. The Cowgirl's Secret Love

Lisa & Josiah Ryder
zoe, mason, jack, expecting
5. The Cowgirl's Forever Love
9. Oh Baby (Vignettes Vol 1)

Julia & Zach Sorenson
anneka
7. The Cowgirl's Chosen Love

The Skyes Family

Petra & Aiden
17. A Cowboy's Bride
jinx, pregnant

Tansy & Jake
18. A Cowboy's Trust
jeffrey

Sydney & Declan
20. A Cowboy's Claim

A NIGHT OF CONTRASTS

A cold wind is blowing through Heart Falls. In some cases, it's not even noticed as things heat up, in more ways than one. But not everyone has found what they need to be warm through and through. Not *yet*.

Featuring: The Stone families: Walker, Ivy & family, Ashton & Sonora, Caleb, Tamara & family, Luke & Kelli, Ginny & Tucker, and Dustin

Timeline: This scene is set the December after **Rose's One Night to Forever**.

1

———

December 29, Heart Falls

cold wind rushed over the bare branches of the larch trees that grew in the fold of the mountain. The snow that had fallen that day swirled skyward as if a genie had tossed an enchantment in the air. The flakes traced the path of the wind as it swooped down toward the foothills then past the small town of Heart Falls.

On the outskirts of town, the lonely shapes of memorial stones buried under snowy hillocks lay in the graveyard. Here everything was quiet. Lives that had been lived to the fullest—or not—everyone here was now equal.

Peaceful. Complete.

Sorrow was there reflected in a fresh bouquet fading under the snow.

Contentment was also represented in the shared names of couples who had passed after twenty, thirty, forty or more years spent walking the earth together.

All now lay silent except for the wind that rustled through the trees lining the edge of the yard.

The small solar lights that dotted the graveyard were covered with snowy caps, creating a magical impression of stars fallen from the sky to land in the quiet place.

A streak of light spilled from the house next door as the back door was shoved open, spotlighting the trampled snow of the backyard. Noise poured out as well, as two children tumbled into the yard, laughing so hard the dog that followed them out burst into an excited chorus of yips that echoed off the nearby headstones.

The wind whirled, spun, and danced around one child as he scooped up snow into a ball and bit down desperately...

INSIDE THE HOUSE, Walker held his hands up even as Ivy pointed a finger at him. "I didn't do anything," he protested.

"It wasn't Daddy," five-year-old Harper agreed. She stood in the doorway watching as her big brother and sister and their still barking dog dragged themselves out of the snow and returned to the porch.

Ivy was on her feet, shaking her head, but amusement shone in her eyes. "Of course, you didn't do anything. Mister One Chip Challenge."

She handed seven-year-old Chloe and nine-year-old Carter each a towel as they reentered the house. "New rule. No matter how hot your mouth gets, you don't get to run outside in the middle of winter without coats or boots."

"Dry your feet," Walker instructed with as much seriousness as he could muster. Then he tugged back the chair beside him and waited for Chloe to return. "I take it you thought that sample was pretty hot?"

Chloe's grin said it all. "Nope. I didn't want Carter to feel left out."

"Hey." Carter blinked then pouted briefly as he settled next to Ivy.

Faithful, the family's golden retriever, bounded over and waited for Harper to sit in her chair again so he could lovingly lay his chin on her leg.

This night wasn't what Walker had expected if he thought back to a year ago. Here he was, playing a game with his family. His *children*.

His gaze met Ivy's. His everything.

She gave him a wink, and that warm spot inside his chest pulsed another time. Contentment and joy bubbled up.

"Everyone ready for the next challenge?" Ivy asked.

Faces went as serious as a gathering of professional poker players. All attention turned to the small takeout container Walker placed in the middle of the table before passing around five clean spoons.

Carter had been the one who had heard about the spicy challenge and decided he wanted to do it for family night. Walker agreed to help organize if Carter went along with a few key changes to make it a little more tender-taste-bud friendly.

Instead of eating a ghost-pepper-or-higher level chip that would've been all about pain and no fun, Walker found increasingly spicy options to offer his children. The bonus part was most of them involved potential meals for the family to enjoy in the future.

Possibly with the heat turned down a little, but who knew how this was going to end?

"So other than the little snowy excursion, everybody okay after eating Uncle Luke's chili?"

"Why's it called chili when it's supposed to be hot?" Harper balanced her elbows on the table as she peered into the new takeout container and took a deep sniff. "This one smells good."

"You think all of them smell good." Carter frowned at his littlest sister. "Is your mouth not on fire?"

"Nope." Harper stuck her spoon in the container then glanced at Walker. "Oops. Sorry, Daddy. I'll wait."

His heart still gave a leap every time he was called daddy.

Walker chuckled. "Looks as if Harper's hungry. This is lamb korma that JP, the cook at Silver Stone, made for us."

Everyone scooped a bit on their spoon. As usual, Chloe was the most cautious, mostly dipping her spoon into the sauce and leaving the meat alone. Ivy took a teeny bit, but Walker knew what he was getting into and scooped up a nice big chunk.

Carter, who wanted nothing better than to imitate Walker, took a heaping spoonful as well.

Walker debated saying something, but the spirit of the game meant he had to keep his mouth shut, and it wasn't as if a little spice would hurt the kid.

It was Chloe's turn. She checked to make sure everybody was armed with a loaded spoon before starting the countdown. "Three, two, one—"

Spoons slipped into mouths, licked clean in an instant, then laid on the table with a crash as per the preestablished rules.

Then the entertainment began.

Across the table from Walker, Carter's eyes widened as he chewed the piece of lamb he'd scooped up with the sauce. He swallowed then opened his mouth, fanning his hand in front of it. "Oh. That's good. Ouch, oh boy."

Ivy rocked in her chair, sipping water as she clearly fought against laughter. "JP will take that as the highest compliment. *Ouch. Oh boy.*"

Carter wrinkled his face at her then flashed a huge grin.

Chloe had put her spoon down at the same time as

everyone else, but she didn't seem to have swallowed her mouthful.

She continued to grimace until Walker took pity on her and offered a quiet reminder. "You don't have to eat it. This is for fun."

She shook her head vigorously, mumbling with her lips still pressed together.

Her choice. All the same, he watched with concern until she took a deep breath, reaching for her glass of grape juice and chugging down almost half of it.

When she did speak it was with great conviction. "Spicy."

"It is," Walker agreed. "Did you like it?"

Chloe wiggled her fingers. "It might be *too* hot."

Across the table, Carter folded his arms across his chest as he examined Harper. She'd swallowed her mouthful and was now scratching Faithful between the eyes as she waited.

"Are you even eating anything?" Carter demanded. "Or are you feeding it to Faithful?"

Walker's youngest daughter looked outraged. "I'm no cheat."

"But you can't be just sitting there. That's impossible."

She stuck out her tongue at him.

Before Walker could intervene, Carter narrowed his gaze.

"Here, try this." Carter grabbed one of the plain tortilla chips that were in bowls around the table meant to nibble on to cool things off. Only he scooped up a healthy serving of the salsa labeled *extra spicy* and passed the chip across the table. "Eat it."

"Carter," Ivy said softly.

Harper wasn't perturbed. "You do it too," she ordered as she accepted the chip from him.

Walker had shared enough meals with his youngest to know exactly what was about to happen. The kid had an iron-lined stomach and a flame-retardant mouth. Why Carter hadn't clued in to this fact yet, Walker had no idea.

Eye to eye as if locked in epic battle, Harper and Carter put the spice-laden chips into their mouth at the same time.

There was no possible way to call a cheat this time.

Five seconds later, Carter's eyes started to water. Ten seconds, and he panted lightly. His little sister, however, calmly swallowed down her chip as if she were lapping up ice cream.

When Harper grabbed the bowl of salsa and the chips and casually scooped up another serving, Carter snorted. "You're impossible."

Harper glanced at Walker. "More spicy things, Daddy?"

"I think Harper wins," Chloe announced, raising her hands and clapping. Then she leaned in close enough to pat her little sister on the back. "But Carter's right. You're impossible."

Faithful barked as if agreeing.

The wind rattled against the door hard enough that Walker got up to make sure the latch was firmly locked. "Spicy challenge is done. Everybody grab a snack bowl, and we'll go watch a show together."

The fact Harper took the chips and salsa with her didn't surprise anyone.

THE WIND SWIRLED AWAY from the little house, the laughter and eager voices fading in the distance as it moved toward the nearby lake.

It paused to rattle the chimney at the house beside the animal rescue. Through the window, an older couple were visible cuddling on a couch in front of a fire. An old dog lay curled up at their feet.

With Ashton's arms around her shoulders, Sonora pressed a

hand to his cheek as she leaned in and touched their lips together.

Another swirl, and the wind crossed the wide meadow toward the nearby ranch. Light shone from the windows at the three main houses and the barn. The soft glow of the yard light over the arena flickered on the snow that had begun to fall.

The man-door to the barn opened. Closed.

Four figures, from a tall woman down to a toddling child, walked slowly together through the darkness. The warm glow of the lantern held in the teenager's hand created an oasis of golden light around them.

Up ahead, the wind hit the main house. The ranch-style building, low and wide, forced the wind to sweep over the roof before sliding past the kitchen window as it cranked open, and the rich scent of chocolate spilled onto the air...

CALEB GLANCED OUT THE WINDOW, swearing as he saw the bobbing light of a lantern halfway between the barn and the house. They were coming back too soon.

He glanced at the oven timer to see three minutes remained.

Resisting the temptation to open the oven door and check on the cookies, a bubbling sound and the scent of something not quite right pulled his attention back to the stovetop.

He jerked the pot of hot chocolate to a different burner and stirred rapidly, leaning down to give a cautious sniff.

"Thank God." He hadn't burnt it.

Another quick peek out the window followed, even as Caleb tried to ignore the rising sense of panic caused by the approaching quartet.

It was just a holiday snack, for heaven's sake. Surely he could manage this for his family.

By the time the mudroom door opened and the cold rushed in, he had successfully poured the hot chocolate into everyone's favourite mugs and lined them up on the counter.

Tamara peered at him over the top of her glasses that had gone foggy after coming in from the cold. "Something smells delicious."

Twelve-year-old Emma kicked off her boots then flung her coat toward a hook. Sasha knelt to help her little brother out of his coat, the fourteen-year-old calling out a protest when Tyler escaped and stomped across the kitchen floor still wearing his boots. "Tyler. No boots in the house."

His news was too big to wait. Tyler threw his arms around Caleb's leg. "Daddy. We saw puppies."

Caleb scooped up the three and a half-year-old, carefully holding him so his dirty boots aimed toward the mudroom and away from the treats. "Puppies. Really?"

"Patchwork Annie is having her babies. Two, so far," Sasha informed him. "Uncle Dustin's taking care of them."

"Well, then, she's in good hands." Caleb passed Tyler to Tamara as the timer went off on the oven. "Everybody with freshly washed hands can have a treat in the living room in two minutes."

Tyler squirmed to be put down, catching hold of Emma's hand and tugging her toward the bathroom. "Emma help," Tyler ordered.

"Of course, Your Majesty." Emma gave Caleb a wink, her blonde curls bouncing as she accompanied Tyler down the hall. Meanwhile, Sasha used the sink in the mudroom, whistling a tune softly as she stared out the window, lost in thought.

At the kitchen sink, Tamara finish washing her hands as Caleb used a spatula to move fresh and gooey chocolate chip cookies to a cooling rack. "This is a nice surprise."

Caleb lifted his shoulders in an easy shrug before leaving his task to come cup her face with both hands. Between the heat of the kitchen and the cold outside, it was a sharp contrast to have her skin against his palms.

He leaned in close. "Sometimes I need to make the world a little sweeter for the most important people I know."

Then he kissed her, warm lips to cool, the heat between them steady and sure. And after the kiss, they spent the next hour together as a family enjoying the treats he'd made. Talking about everything and nothing. Plans for the coming year, puppies and kittens, and baby goats—*dear God.*

As the children before him laughed and Tamara's eyes sparkled at him, Caleb counted his blessings.

He truly was a lucky man.

The wind increased in volume as it carried a lingering warmth across the lake, snowflakes whirling in circles, swooping left and right. The lights of the newer home on the far side of Big Sky Lake shone off the clear icy surface while freezing temperatures crept frosty fingers around the edges of the bathroom window.

A steam-covered window that suddenly had a hand pressed to the middle. Palm sliding down the foggy surface as a low moan rattled the glass...

"Holy hell, that was amazing." Kelli twisted, separating their bodies for long enough to spear her fingers into Luke's hair and pull him to his feet. He went reluctantly, still tasting her pleasure on his lips.

He crowded her against the door, her naked skin pressed to

his fully clothed body like a wicked daydream come to life. He'd caught her in the middle of taking a shower, and watching hadn't been enough. Thankfully, she'd laughed as he'd hauled her from the shower stall and into his arms.

Going down on her in the bathtub area had been a spectacular natural progression.

Kelli stroked her fingers through his hair. "Thanks for that lovely interlude."

"My line." He kissed her gently. "Damn, I can't get enough of you."

"You're like a wild man tonight."

"Construction is officially finished. You said we should celebrate," he reminded her, his gaze drifting over her body as he let every bit of his fiery need for her show. "Which means sex. Against every wall, every door, on every fucking floor."

And then he wasn't talking because his mouth was on hers, the hand behind her head capturing her in place so he could consume her.

Even as she kissed him back, wild and wet and sweet, Kelli dug her fingernails into his shoulders. The sharp bite sent a lightning zap along his nerve endings and upped the urgency to move. He needed her as much now as he had in the beginning.

A second later he had her swung up into his arms.

She curled her arms around his neck. "Which wall first?"

Fuck that. The truth was he didn't have the patience for gymnastics tonight. "Walls later. Now I want you under me, screaming my name."

"Fireplace?"

Hell, yes. Luke all but jogged to the area, Kelli laughing the entire time.

They'd been brilliant when they'd designed the house, even though some had questioned why they basically had two living spaces almost on top of each other.

One was a living room, a place for family and friends to gather. This cozy space to the side, with two easy chairs and a more intimate setting, was for him and Kelli. They had a fire in the airtight stove every morning, with quiet conversations and plenty of time to grow together.

Bonus? It had turned out to be a fantastic spot to get down and dirty.

Kelli's amusement was clear, but so was the heat in her eyes as he carefully lowered her feet to the floor in front of the fire he'd lit after supper.

She curled her fingers into the material of his T-shirt and tugged him toward her. "You need to be naked."

"Only parts of me," he pointed out, waggling his brows.

"All of you," she corrected, brushing her lips over his with a promise of more. "I want to see everything. The way firelight looks on that sexy body of yours should be illegal."

"Oh?" Luke ripped off his shirt and tossed it aside. He grabbed her hand and pressed it to his chest. "I hope you need to look really close."

"Absolutely." Kelli traced a finger down his chest, lingering on his stomach muscles.

A shiver rolled over his skin. God, what this woman did to him.

She undid the button on his jeans, unzipping them just far enough to slip her hand under the fabric and cup his cock.

Luke moaned. "Fuck."

A soft laugh escaped her as she magically kept hold of him and eased his jeans off his hips. They fell to the floor, and he somehow kicked them off even as Kelli adjusted her grip to stroke more firmly.

Pleasure jumbled through him at her touch, at the soft stroke of her skin under his palms as he filled his hands with her breasts. Kelli threw the soft quilt off her chair to the floor, and they ended up on it in a tangle of limbs and lips.

Need and desire, heated touches and passionate kisses, all bathed in firelight glow. Kelli straddled him and eased herself onto his shaft.

They both groaned. Then their gazes met, and they laughed.

Luke's hands fisted on her hips as Kelli undulated over him. The feel of her sex surrounding him was everything physical sensation could offer, but it was the *more* that made this perfect.

The laughter in her voice, the care in her touch. The little sounds that escaped her as he rocked upward and met her stroke for stroke.

The trust between them. Growing bigger and bigger every moment, every day, every year.

"I love you." He said the words while staring into her face.

Her eyes brightened just seconds before she gasped, head falling back as her pussy tightened down on him with a demand he couldn't ignore. He gave in to the release that tore out of him with a heat that all but melted his bones.

Kelli draped herself over him, the fire crackling nearby. Their breath still ragged, but contentment a blanket that covered them with as much heat as the fire.

SPARKS FLEW UP *the chimney and out into the night. Caught by the wind, they danced for a few brief moments before dying. The ashes were carried on the wind toward the small cottage across from the other two homes. Here the mood was far more somber...*

. . .

Tucker stirred the soup in the pot on the stove and tried not to get caught constantly peeking at Ginny. It was tough, though. So tough.

She looked as if she'd been run over by a herd of horses.

His Ginny, always so full of vim and vigour, sat curled up in the corner of the couch. She held a book in her hands, but during the last ten minutes her head had tilted sideways, eyelids falling closed.

She'd barely eaten any supper, and she'd been sleeping terribly. Nothing made a man feel more powerless than not being able to help the woman he loved.

Tucker stuck his finger into the soup to check it for temperature before pouring it into a mug. Also, nothing was worse than catching a cold over the holiday season.

Of course, that's if it *was* a cold…

Mug in hand, he settled on the coffee table in front of her, staring at her face, the warm lights of the fire reflecting off the reddish tinge in her hair. Yeah, she looked exhausted.

He'd never been more in love with her. More convinced that she was beautiful, through and through.

"I can feel you staring at me." Ginny cracked one eye open. She watched him silently for a minute then wiped a hand across her lips. "If I was drooling, you're not allowed to tell me that."

He reached forward, exchanging the warm soup for the book he stole from her fingers. "If you had been drooling, I would tease you mercilessly. But alas, nothing from you but the cutest little snores."

Ginny snorted. "Get out."

"Not so little snores?"

She rolled her eyes, but more importantly, she lifted the mug to her lips and took a cautious sip. Her nose wrinkled, but she swallowed. "Nice and warm."

"You cold?"

When he would have gotten up to grab her a blanket or put more wood on the fire, she glared at him. "I can be warm enough and still say something warm is nice. Stop babying me."

"Okay, okay." He held up his hands in agreement.

But he watched her. Closely. Because…

Screw it. If he was wrong, then maybe she was truly sick, and she'd be too weak to kill him.

Tucker reached under the couch and pulled out a plastic bag. "Speaking of babies…"

He sat there, motionless. The package extended forward while Ginny's eyes grew as big as saucers.

Yeah, well, she'd said the word first, not him. He nudged the bag at her. "It's a test kit."

She didn't move. Just clung to her mug like it was a life preserver and she'd found herself in the middle of the Pacific Ocean.

"A test kit to find out if you're pregnan—"

"I figured that part out," Ginny informed him, still not taking the package. "I don't need it."

Tucker folded his arms over his chest. "Why are you doing this? Which, by the way, your sister Dare totally warned me you would do."

That got Ginny moving. She put her mug aside and leaned forward, red finally colouring her cheeks. "You talked to Dare about me needing a pregnancy test?"

"Not recently," Tucker admitted. "But since we haven't been using birth control for six months, and you told Dare *that* less than twenty-four hours after we decided to ditch it, yes, I've had a couple conversations about pregnancy and tests and etcetera with her. Each of which I told you about and you'd remember if you weren't so befuddled right now."

"But I *am* befuddled, and it's *just. A. Cold,*" Ginny all but shouted before pressing her hands to the sides of her head. "Oh my God, I'm an idiot."

Tucker was at her side a second later, arm draped around her shoulders. Surrounding her as best he could, holding her tenderly. "You are *not* an idiot, but you are either sick or possibly pregnant. And since it would be good to know which, do you think you can go pee on the nice present I bought you?"

She snickered softly, nuzzling her face into the curve of his neck. "I'm sorry I yelled."

"It's okay. I get it."

"Yeah, well, maybe it's me who's *got it* this time." She snickered again. "I do want a baby with you. I haven't been obsessing over it, though. Just figured we can keep having fun and it'll happen when it happens."

He squeezed her shoulders, pressing a kiss to the top of her head. To her forehead. Tilting her face up so he could kiss along her jaw. "It has been fun, and if you're not pregnant, we'll keep having fun. Also, not just to get you pregnant. I like sex with you, Ginny Stewart."

"Ditto, Tucker Stewart." She reached down and picked up the plastic bag. Peered in. "Okay. Let's go find out if I'm drinking chicken noodle soup for my cold or diving into pickles and ice cream."

Tucker stood and pulled her to her feet, tucking her against his body and savouring the warmth and the way she leaned into him, hands curled around his biceps. "Either way, I love you. I'm here for you."

"I know." She took a deep breath. "Let's do it."

The wind outside whistled against the rafters, a soft tone that made the inside of the house feel safe. Home.

Ginny took his hand, lifted the test kit, and tugged him toward the bathroom.

. . .

Softer now, the wind eased. The temperature leveled out as a thick layer of clouds rolled in overhead. Covering the sky, the grey and black clouds turned the night sky into a solid, starless canvas. Nothing to see, no trace of light, as if waiting for the next brush strokes to fall and continue the story.

One final gust rattled the barn door hard enough that it sprang open, the children not having pulled it tight. The cold outside a harsh contrast against the warm animal-scented air in the barn...

Dustin sprang to his feet and hurried to push the door shut, the cold spinning into the barn deep enough to make him shiver.

He stopped for a moment despite the temperature to stare up into the sky. Dark, blank.

Lonely.

Enough. Shutting the door firmly, he strolled back to the stall where Patchwork Annie had decided to have her pups. Probably didn't need to supervise, but he was on night duty, and the border collie was special.

Dustin had *liberated* the beast from his uncle's ranch a year earlier. She adored him, and Annie was his more than any of the other working dogs around the Silver Stone ranch. Hell, he had the bill to prove it.

She glanced up as he settled on a nearby bale. Close, but not too close. So far, Annie was doing just fine without his help, curled up in the warm nest made of clean straw and a couple of blankets he'd brought for her. A row of three puppies nestled against her belly, with maybe one or two more to come.

In a while he'd go and work through the list that Tucker and Ashton had left for him. But the night was young, and his shift wasn't over until six a.m. There was no reason he couldn't linger a bit longer.

He leaned back against the stall wall, propped his boots up on another bale and stared into the rafters. No reason he couldn't be the one to work nights most of the time.

There was no one for him to go home to.

Pity party, much?

Dustin shook his head. Yeah, maybe it was stupid, but he had to admit he wanted what his brothers and sister had—someone who was theirs, through and through, for all the right reasons. He might be young, but he'd seen how happy his siblings were. He'd watched them build those connections over the past years.

Only made sense to want that same happiness for himself. To want to give like that to another person...someday.

Patchwork Annie made a soft noise. Dustin snapped his attention off his musings and back on her. "Hey, darling. You okay?"

She wagged her tail as he settled beside her, the pups a small mass of warmth under his palm. He stayed close for another hour until all the puppies had arrived, then brushed Annie's head gently.

"I need to get to work. You done good, mama," he told her after leaving her fresh water and a snack near at hand.

Annie rested her head on her paws and let out an enormous sigh. Contentment in every inch of her as the six pups lined up at her teats wiggled and squirmed as they nursed.

Dustin chuckled as he rose, humming softly as he began his chores. A night working in the quiet of the barns was on his agenda.

And for now, it was enough.

If you'd like to find out what comes next for Dustin, and how he finds the perfect person to share his world with, **A Rancher's Vow** is the final book in the Stone of Heart Falls series.

SEIZE THE MOMENT

Weddings are always fun, and family weddings even better. But with everyone high on matrimonial fumes, and her entire family working hard to convince she's up next in the wedding department, Petra needs a distraction. Someone she doesn't know and will never see again for a decidedly non-getting-hitched end to the evening.

Another stranger in Heart Falls for only a night, Aiden's perfect for some physical, happy-hormonal party-time. A knight-in-shining armour who kisses like a god? One night is all Petra needs.

Featuring: Petra Sorenson, Zach & Julia Sorenson and the entire Sorenson family, and introducing Aiden Skye

. . .

Timeline: This scene is set in September during the final pages of **The Cowgirl's Chosen Love** the day of Julia and Zach's second wedding. (First wedding in Vegas they don't remember —it's complicated.)

1

———

PETRA

As far as weddings went, Petra had to admit this one was pretty awesome.

It wasn't only the venue, although the location didn't hurt one bit.

The vista to the west of Red Boot ranch was full of rolling foothills gliding up to the dramatic heights of the Alberta Rocky Mountains. The late September weather was perfect, and the sky overhead was a robin egg blue so bright it almost hurt her eyes.

The arbour where Petra's brother, Zach, and his almost wife for the second time, Julia, stood exchanging their vows was also over-the-top perfection with garlands of flowers and greenery woven through the wooden trellis. The entire setting was something out of a spectacular movie set.

But the real reason today was knocking her socks off were the people. When it came to family lotteries, she had won.

Of course, sometimes with all her siblings older than her—four sisters and then Zach—Petra sometimes had to work really hard to find alone time.

But today, as the wedding moved on from the vow exchanges to a delicious dinner and then dancing, there wasn't much about her world that Petra would change.

"Guess we'll be doing this for you someday soon," brother-in-law one teased as he danced her around the floor.

"You guys have all got the marital bliss thing down pat, so someday, but not yet." Petra smiled at him. Her sister had made a good match and the two of them had already created a passel of kids. "For now I'm happy to be the solo Sorenson. It's up to me to come up with wild and crazy things to set you all gossiping on the family chat."

He grinned and twirled her, amusement there as if he knew she would never do anything scandalous. "Well, once we're back home, I'll have to introduce you to some of the single guys in IT at the shop."

Petra hurried to reassure him she had no need of matchmaking skills, but obviously with wedding fumes in the air, there was no stopping it.

Brother-in-law number two spun her on the dance floor and made an offer of a similar nature. "Pat's a really good guy. He was divorced about four years ago, so he's not on a rebound or anything. He was asking about you."

She eyed Ronan hard. "Why would he have been asking about me?"

He had the grace to look a little sheepish. "Might've been showing off some family pictures and you were in there."

Good grief. "Pictures from when?"

Yes, he definitely grimaced this time. "Hawaii."

If they hadn't been dancing, Petra would've pinched the bridge of her nose. "Let me guess. You were taking pictures of the kids being adorable and doing cannonballs into the pool, and I *happened* to be suntanning somewhere in the vicinity."

"Swore I cropped you out," he insisted. "I wasn't trying to

show you off. Just so proud of my family, and that means you as well."

Truth was Petra knew he meant every word.

Even when brother-in-law number three informed her he had met the best group of people at the local rec center, and had she ever considered getting involved in Tai Chi? Petra knew the meddling came from a place of love.

Brother-in-law number four wasn't even subtle about it. "We want you to be as happy as we are," Drew offered.

"Oh, I know. And I get it, but someday, not today." She tipped her head toward where Zach and Julia swayed slowly, ignoring the more rapid beat of the music. "Today is about them and how happy we are for them. That's why we're here as a whole family. Really, it's enough. I promise."

Drew let her go and nodded, grin widening. "We'll wait until the weekend's over."

Jackass. "Was that a promise or a threat?" she tossed after him as he returned to his wife.

Suddenly Zach was there, holding his hand out. "I think it's my turn for a dance, little sis."

"I can't believe you unpeeled yourself from Julia," she teased even as he led her onto the floor, dancing with brotherly appropriateness.

"Dad stole her away," Zach complained. "I figured I was supposed to dance with Mom, but she sent me over to you."

"So I'm your backup choice?"

He snorted. "Sorry, kiddo. My brain is obviously not firing on all cylinders. No, I absolutely want to dance with you. Good chance to say thank you for everything you've done to welcome Julia into the family."

"It wasn't hard," Petra informed him. "She's one in a million. I'm really pleased for you, big bro."

Happiness poured off him before a momentary crease

formed between his brows. "This probably means some of the horde will start poking you about settling down."

A laugh burst free. "Some? Try every single one of them, via lines of brother-in-law communication."

"Dammit, don't listen to that shit. You're damn smart. You'll find the right somebody when it's time," he said with conviction. "Because I really do want this for you, but *you'll* know when it's right."

"That's what I figured," Petra agreed as she let him lead. She tilted her head toward the side of the room where Julia now stood talking with their mom and dad. "I've had a lot of good examples. I'll follow in your footsteps," she promised.

"Well, maybe not the accidentally getting married part... It turned out well, but it was hellish at times." The music stopped, and Zach stood back and offered his elbow. "Maybe avoid the whole fake-relationship thing as well. It made things complicated from the get-go."

"No fake boyfriend, no pretend engagements. I will remain on the straight and narrow when it comes to relationships."

He patted her fingers where they lay on his arm. "Now let's see how the fates mess that up for you."

Which meant they were both laughing when they arrived next to their parents and Julia.

A question flashed in Julia's eyes, but she didn't have time to ask anything before Zach twirled her back onto the dance floor.

Petra's parents waited. Her mother raised a brow.

Petra grinned. "Zach is laying odds of how much weirder my in-the-far-future hookup with a boyfriend/partner will be than his."

Pamela clicked her tongue for a second. "I told the children they were *not* allowed to start any betting pools, and certainly not post anything in the family chatroom until after the weekend."

Oh my God. "Seriously. You've already had that discussion with them, yet I still got a *let me help you find a good man* from every one of them?"

Zachary Senior waved a hand in the air as if brushing off flies. "If you weren't so strong and independent, we'd worry. But all that teasing probably means you've gotten your back up and will do exactly what you planned to in the first place." He dipped his chin firmly. "Good for you."

Impulsively, she wrapped her arms around her parents and squeezed tightly. "I love you, both. And yes, you raised some fine people, albeit nosy and a little too tightly connected at times."

"Backhanded compliments are the best," Pamela said with a smile before turning to her husband. "It's our turn to get out there for a while, don't you think?"

There were enough other guests at the wedding Petra got pulled onto the dance floor more than enough times to not feel left out. They held the gift unwrapping, ate a late supper, then went back on the dance floor for more.

Suddenly, it was eleven thirty. Petra stood at the side of the room sipping on a lemonade as her gaze drifted over a sea of people that included the enormous wave of her own family. Sisters one through four were all represented on the floor, husbands turning and twisting them like perfectly content cake toppers. Mom and Dad had gone out again, and in the center of the room, staring at each other as if they were the only people in the world, Zach and Julia.

Petra sipped her drink and soaked in happiness. Until, out of the blue, something struck that was not quite...

Well, she could honestly say it wasn't jealousy because

she'd been telling the truth. She wanted what they had, but not *now*. Another more careful glance around the room and some intense thinking shed light on the other part that she *did* want here and now.

A whole lot of people had somebody they were going home with tonight.

And not that she wanted to think too hard about her family and sex, it was natural. As her mother insisted with her far too blunt conversations, sex really did make the world go on.

Ignoring the parts of *that* particular bunny trail that made her brain get squicky, Petra focused on the fixable problem. Maybe she was pumped up on emotion. Maybe there were pheromones in the air, but she was definitely running hot, because the instant she thought about finding someone to enjoy a different sort of dancing with, her mind set on a solution.

Saturday night in Heart Falls? Rough Cut pub was right there. She could be on the dance floor in under fifteen minutes, and the place didn't close until two.

Some dirtier dancing with someone not related to her...

If she was very, *very* lucky she'd find someone perfectly happy to help her enjoy her own pleasure-filled night.

It was a moment's work to slip from the party pavilion. She was already dressed up, her pretty wedding dress only a little fancier than she'd usually wear to go out. Her hair was good, her make up as much as she ever wore.

The pile of coats that had accumulated in the room her family had taken over caused a brief problem when she couldn't easily spot her purse.

"Thank God there's an app for that." Petra snickered at herself as she opened her phone and cued up the AirTag finder. After too many lost purses and bags over the years, Petra had given up being embarrassed by her bad habit and gone with the flow.

She dug straight to the source, looped her purse over her shoulder, and made her escape. She sent mental waves of happiness and love back to her family, but what she was hoping for now was a physical sexual escapade hot enough to make her see stars.

2

———————

AIDEN

*A*iden Skye swallowed the last bite of his burger then washed it down with a swig of a decent local brew, the growing sense of *rightness* sinking in deep.

Heart Falls was exactly what he'd been looking for.

As the Saturday night crowd flowed across the dance floor in Rough Cut pub, he mentally did one final shift through the list of requirements and could honestly say every box had been checked. Heart Falls was small enough to stay under the radar, yet close enough to a big city to be able to access everything they'd need and reach the people who needed it.

It would take them a couple of years to be ready to move, but this was the first, all-important step. Finding the perfect spot to locate their rescue ranch.

While Heart Falls already had an animal rescue, they planned to quietly focus on people. To create a safe place for those who needed a brief getaway en route to a better life and give them a chance to get their feet under them. A place for ladies to escape bad home situations they didn't deserve to be in.

Right now, it was all one big, glorious dream, but the details would come. Aiden and his brothers, Declan and Jake—especially Jake—would get the details in place. Jake wanted out of his career in law enforcement, and Declan...

Declan insisted that having a new goal to focus on would only help as he mourned his wife. A terrible situation that would lead to something good and powerful.

For now, this was Aiden's job. They knew they wanted to be somewhere in the area, and he lived the closest. Since the spring, he'd been taking his free days off work to explore all the small towns in southern Alberta. He finally hit Heart Falls, and another shot of *this is right* slammed into him.

Oh, there was a whole lot more they needed to do, but at least knowing where to aim was a good start.

Aiden turned his attention to the dance floor, preparing to enjoy a couple of hours of pleasurable distraction. His motel room was on the small size, and while it was comfortable and clean, he didn't need to head there until after closing time.

He spotted her the instant she walked into the room. She power-walked as if she'd installed a new set of batteries, bouncing with each step. Eagerness flitted in her eyes as she positioned herself to the side of the room and surveyed the dancers.

Tall and leggy—damn, he liked them leggy. Her dark brown hair was done up fancy-like, with ringlets off her temples and the rest of it in curling swoops that played around her shoulders.

Aiden had a sudden dire need to see that shiny hair laid out on his pillow.

He eased to his feet and headed her direction.

Suddenly, she hustled toward him, gaze still mostly on the dance floor. Halfway between them, an oversized cowboy chatting with his buddies raised his beer high and tipped sideways, backing directly into her path.

Aiden was too far away to stop the collision, but he dashed forward quickly enough to tuck an arm around her waist and spin her aside before anything more than a slight bump and redirection occurred.

He held her close, twisting her to safety before making eye contact with the big bruiser who glared at them even as he caught his balance.

"Hey, buddy," Aiden offered cheerfully. "You okay?"

The man took a minute to focus then waggled his head from side to side. "Sorry, lady. I need to take a piss."

He rumbled off at high speed, head down and intent on his destination.

The woman in Aiden's arms snickered, patting a hand on his chest. "And that is the definition of a cowboy. Honest and blunt to the core."

"And thankfully out of reach of stepping on our toes." He shuffled them to the side a little farther without loosening his hold completely. She remained leaning toward him, hand on his chest. Her fingertips moved in circles instead of pushing him away. "Don't want you taking a tumble."

"Thank you for rescuing me," she smiled at him prettily. "So, stranger. Do you dance as well as you rescue maidens in distress?"

Hallelujah. He tilted his head toward the crowd, stepping back far enough to offer his hand. "One of my favourite things."

She slid her fingers into his and they headed onto the floor. For the next three songs they moved together with an ease that defied explanation. The rapid two step didn't leave him breath to more than exchange their names but spinning her around the room was treat enough.

When the fourth dance song slowed, Aiden kept her in

tight, not willing to give her up so easily. "Need a break? Drink?"

She eased even closer, slipping her fingers around the back of his neck and lining them up tight. "I want to keep dancing. I'm being greedy and keeping you all to myself."

"Ain't being greedy if it's freely offered." He kept the hand on her lower back where it was, resisting the temptation to go down for a scoop of her soft ass. Maybe if the evening continued to go this well, he'd get a chance for that in private.

Pale-blue eyes met his gaze. "So, cowboy. You live around here?"

"Nope. Just passing through and decided to come looking for some charming company. How about you? You look as if you know the place."

Something glinted in her eyes. "I come through here every now and then, but I live in Manitoba. Close to the family farm."

She said it in such a way that made it clear she didn't mind one bit. He liked that.

"You get along good with your family?"

A laugh burst free from her red-tinted lips. "Sometimes too well. You?"

"Love my brothers. We've been off in different directions for a couple years, but we're planning on relocating in one spot in the future so we can work together again."

"Good for you," she said sincerely. Aiden danced her away from a near collision, and she curled into him tighter, accepting the quick adjustment without a fight.

"You want to talk about our jobs?" he asked, desire growing steadily as her body swayed the slightest bit more than necessary, rubbing them together in a sweet yet dirty promise.

"How about we talk about other things? Like, do you want to kiss me?" Petra stared him in the eye.

Challenge accepted. Swaying gently, he lowered his head until their lips brushed. One time, and another, the taste of her flooding his senses. The sweetness of her lip gloss and the bright taste of lust mingled as her tongue teased his for a fleeting second.

He pulled away before it went too far, because while he had no problem with public displays of affection, there was no need to broadcast where this might be going.

Petra, happily, seemed on board with where his thoughts were headed. She took a deep breath and laid her hand on his shoulder, tall enough they were nearly eye to eye. "The man can kiss. Is it too much to hope that means you have other skills?"

He chuckled. "I like a woman who knows enough to do test runs before starting anything." He tucked his fingers under her chin. "We moved together pretty good here on the dance floor. If we head somewhere else, like my motel room, my first goal is to make you feel good. What comes after that is just gravy on the biscuit."

3

PETRA

*I*f Petra had been getting high on happiness fumes before, she was even hotter now that lust had kicked in.

There was something so enticing about being in a man's arms when he clearly knew how to make a woman feel good. It wasn't that he was slick, saying all the right things and teasing her in the right ways, but as they slipped out the door of Rough Cut hand-in-hand, Petra decided this felt too right to worry about.

Her body buzzed like crazy with building need.

Aiden pulled them to a stop outside the doors of Rough Cut, pushing her shoulders against the wood paneling and taking her lips again. She was getting drunk on the taste of him.

He broke away, eyes shining down at her. "There somebody you want to send a note to, darlin'? We're headed to the Heart Falls motel, room fourteen. My name's Aiden Skye—sky with an e—they've got all my info at the check-in."

"Safe and consensual. Very sexy." Petra wasn't about to message any of her usual friends or contacts, but thankfully, with her IT skills, staying safe was simple enough. She pulled out her phone and set up an alert. She snapped a picture of Aiden and added it to the text.

He didn't need to know that nothing would go out unless she didn't shut off the alert in the morning.

It wasn't as if she wanted anyone to come looking for her before then anyway.

She tucked her phone away, grabbed him by the collar, hovering her lips just over his. "Details mostly done. Condom. We will use one."

He chuckled, stroking his knuckles down the line of her jaw. "Oh, ye of little faith. I have more than one, and we'll use them all."

Petra laughed. "Good thing I've been doing my exercises."

He took her mouth again, and this time it wasn't one of the needy but teasing ones like on the dance floor. This was hunger and possession, toe curling and electrifying.

When he straightened slightly, elbows leaning on the wall on either side of her head, heavy exhales escaped his lips in rapid succession, and there was a slightly dazed expression in his eyes. "Holy shit, woman. You are going to rock my—"

She wiggled out from under him, caught him by the wrist, and pulled him down the street. "Less talking, more walking," she ordered.

It still took fifteen minutes to complete the five-minute walk. He tugged her to a stop, slid his hand to the back of her waist, and pulled their bodies into full contact as he kissed her slow and deliberately. A moment later, when Petra spotted what she thought was a familiar car coming down the road, she drew Aiden with her into the shadows beside the drugstore. This time he was against the building, grinning down at her. She pressed up against him and curled a hand around the back of his neck to bring their mouths in contact.

When he finally held his key card to the hotel door and it sprang open, Petra barely had time to glance around the neatly arranged room. A small duffle bag sat on the dresser, and a coat hung from the hook on the wall.

Then Aiden was between her and the view, his devilish smile lighting her up and giving her even more dangerous ideas.

"Your lips are damn addictive," he said huskily. "I'm kind of scared to take a taste of the rest of you because there might be no coming back from this."

She planted a hand on his chest, hurriedly undoing the buttons of his shirt. "Ditto."

A wild scramble ensued. Petra didn't remember ever being so on fire for someone. She pushed the shirt off his shoulders, and he lifted her dress over her head. Her bra was off in an instant, and he swore softly as his hands came up to cup her breasts.

As good as it felt to have him squeezing and teasing, his fingertips brushing circles over her nipples, the ache between her legs grew more insistent, as if there were a timer involved. She undid his jeans button and slid down the zipper, then found herself rising in the air and carried to the bed. Pants stripped away, shoes tossed aside, Aiden did the world's fastest strip, and then they were together on the bed, naked skin to naked skin, his hands roaming over her with an urgency she felt as well.

He slipped his fingers between her legs as he put their lips together and kissed her.

There was nothing but sensation. The hot fire of the kiss and the demanding touch, his fingers playing over her clit. Stroking, teasing, and driving her upward until she hovered on the edge, ready to tip too quickly, too soon.

"Let go, Petra. I'll make you feel good over and over. All night. I got this."

Petra rocked her hips into his touch, and he pressed a little harder as she broke. Pleasure radiated out from her core, and she arched her entire body against his.

Before she was anywhere near done, he was there, condom in place, tip at her core. He cupped her chin bringing her eyes to his. "Yes?"

"Yes. Now."

He slipped in. Not a pounding thrust, but a slow, relentless conquering that set off a series of aftershocks. When Aiden cursed, smile on his lips, she laughed, lifting her legs around his hips to draw him deeper into her body. "Harder. Do it," she demanded.

Aiden obliged. He set up a rhythm, connecting them over and over, not too fast, not too slow. He leaned on his left elbow, lifting off her body enough for room to ease his hand back down her torso, playing with her breasts so perfectly Petra gasped in the rush of sensation.

He slipped his hand between her legs, perfectly aligned so that the additional contact with her clit made her orgasm flare again. She didn't think it had ever stopped.

"I'd ask if it was good, but you feel like fucking heaven."

"No, you're fucking Petra," she teased, gasping as he pinched her clit, and suddenly she was unable to speak or tease or do anything except to contain a scream. Pleasure brushed over her, so big and insistent there was no chance of her controlling it. She dug her heels into his butt and accepted the pleased grin on his face as his due.

The spark in his eyes got wilder, and his pace picked up, desperation gliding over his expression until he jerked to a stop, head thrown back, body rigid.

Inside her, Petra felt his cock jerk, felt the tension of his pleasure in the rigid muscles of his body under her fingers as they clung together through every last pulse of the orgasm.

She'd made a good choice. This was one fine way to celebrate.

Aiden cupped her cheek, smiling at her brightly. "Gotta take care of things, but don't go anywhere."

Petra unwrapped herself from him. "No plans to move farther than a few feet. Got a water, though? We might need to hydrate for you to do that more than once."

Which meant Aiden was laughing as he rolled off the bed, headed to the bathroom to take care of the condom. "There's water in the cooler in the corner," he offered. "I'll grab it for you in a second. Don't want you passing out from dehydration."

"Might pass out from other better reasons," Petra said.

That was the first. Aiden came back to the bed and demanded she roll over. An impromptu massage turned into him going down on her and licking until she panted so hard with pleasure she nearly did pass out.

They napped, tangled together, waking up to go at it again. When Petra's alarm went off at 5:30 a.m., Aiden blinked a moment and then opened his arms and let her out. "Heading home?"

She nodded. "I'll be back before the family knows I was gone." She smiled down at him. "You were exactly what I needed. Thank you, kind sir, for sharing your bed. And your tongue. And your mighty fine cock."

Aiden laughed as he folded his hands behind his head. "You're welcome to said company, fingers, and cock, and thank you, as well." He watched her as she dressed and pulled her hair up into a messy bun. Thoughtful. "Give me a second. I'll walk you back to your vehicle."

She waved for him to stay in bed. "Not that I deliberately planned it this way, but there was no room in the Rough Cut parking lot, so I parked here. I'm less than ten paces away."

He snorted. "Okay, then."

She had barely opened the door when Aiden stopped her.

"Petra." She glanced back, and he pointed at the chair where her purse still lay, phone beside it. "Don't forget those."

For heaven's sake. "Thanks. That would have made life more complicated." She snatched them up, blew him a quick kiss, and quietly left.

Back in her truck, she deleted the warning message she'd scheduled then headed back to Red Boot ranch.

Petra caught herself grinning. She'd had a one night stand. Aiden Skye was a good man, and she wished him the best of luck in the future.

Spending the night with a total stranger wasn't something she planned to do on a regular basis, but it had been exactly what she needed. Not a moment to find forever but one to seize, with pleasurable company and a few really good orgasms.

Petra was completely content.

For now.

IF YOU'D LIKE to find out what happens a few years later, and how Petra and Aiden re-meet and fall in love, check out **A Cowboy's Bride**. It's the first book in the Skyes of Heart Falls series.

WEDDING IN A BOX

Petra and Aiden got married without much fanfare for all the right reasons.

It does mean they have no *official day of the wedding* pictures, so they've come up with a special way to commemorate getting hitched. We get to visit with some Heart Falls favourites as they follow the special photo instructions (and share some important moments with us!)

Featuring: Caleb & Tamara Stone, Karen & Finn Marlette (and the Coleman sisters and their children), Petra & Aiden Skye

Timeline: This story is set in March during **A Cowboy's Trust.**

INTRODUCTION

March 1.
Email to family and friends from Petra and Aiden Skye

Hello, everyone! We're excited to invite you to be part of our fun wedding project! We'd love for you to take a special photo for us, following the steps below:

1. Find Your Box

Use a large, plain cardboard box (see size on attached PDF) that will be big enough to fit one or two people's torsos inside. Make sure it's neutral (brown, white, etc.) and doesn't have any logos or distracting patterns. No, Papa Sorenson, you don't need to ship anything to all of us—just recycle and reuse! Fold in the top and bottom so you have a see-through tube.

2. Pose in the Box

Get creative! We want to see fun, quirky, or romantic poses of you inside the box. Feel free to act like you're popping out of the box, leaning on the edge, tossing snowflakes or frisbees! Fun expressions encouraged as if you were celebrating at our wedding! Solo, as a couple, or as a family—your call.

You can even decorate the front edge of the box if you'd like (think hearts, flowers, etc.), but keep it simple so you're the focus.

3. Dress Up or Dress Down

Wear something fun! You can go fancy, in wedding-worthy attire, or keep it casual and playful. If you have props (flowers, hats, or anything wedding-related), feel free to include them. We'll be wearing something nice, but nothing formal, if you feel the need to follow suit. Only rule—NO clowns. (Seriously, Tansy, why is that the first place your brain went? You're terrible.)

4. Take the Picture

Position the box on a table or however works best.

Make sure there's good lighting (natural light is great!) and the whole box is visible in the photo. If possible, take the picture against a plain background for best results.

5. Send It In

When you're happy with your photo, send it to Petra. Yes, the bride is taking care of the photos. The computer geek in her is delighted!

We can't wait to see your creative takes and include your photo in our special wedding collection. Once it's put together, we'll be sure to link to the images so you can upload your own copies of the final portraits.

Thanks for being part of our memories. We'll host the official wedding party this summer!

Petra and Aiden Skye

47

1

CALEB

Stepping in the door, Caleb came to a complete and utter halt with one foot still on the snowy stoop. In front of him, half hidden by a cardboard box, was a familiar silhouette wearing Tamara's slippers. Mostly, though, all he could see of his wife was her sweet ass.

"*Christ.*"

She jerked upright, twirling on the spot. The box dropped until it was draped over her shoulders like a misshapen shawl. "Caleb. You scared the hell out of me."

He eyed her, closing the door as he stepped into the room. "Is this some new viral trend I'm not aware of?"

She frowned before hauling the box over her head. "Oh, this?"

"If it's fashion, I don't get it," he pointed out dryly. "Or if it's a box, it's not a very good one."

"Depends on what you want it for." Her lips twitched. "It's perfect for taking pictures in."

Nope. She'd lost him again. He toed off his boots so he

could return to the more important reason that had him hightailing it into the house. "Spotted the kids in the barn."

"Jinx came over, so Sasha and Emma decided they all needed to go on a kitten hunt with Tyler."

That was what he'd heard from the group when he met them. Which also meant he knew how little time they had without children in the house.

Caleb reached for the box, examining it closer. "Are those fabric flowers? On the edge of the...?" He shook his head. It didn't matter that his wife was doing something strange with Amazon boxes. Not at this moment, anyway. "Never mind."

He placed the surprisingly sturdy cardboard aside and caught Tamara by the hand.

She raised a brow. "Yes?"

"I need you."

She looked around then checked the wall clock. "Okay. What for?"

Fighting a laugh, Caleb tugged her sharply. She smacked into his body, breasts hitting his chest and hips tight to his. She stayed there because he instantly put a hand to her lower back and pinned her in place.

Amusement danced over her face. "Well, now. Let me rephrase that. *Where* do you need me?"

As much as he wished they could drop everything, being responsible adults meant escorting her down the hall to the bedroom, just in case the kitten hunt got called off early. "You don't mind me interrupting your rousing activity with the cardboard box?"

Tamara twisted to walk backward so she could tug his shirt free from his jeans and help him strip it over his head. "Boxy will be there when I'm ready for him."

"You named it?" Caleb crowded her in the door, closed and

locked it, then pressed her against the solid wood. "That's all sorts of wrong."

Tamara cupped his face in her hands, lowering her chin and offering her best sultry stare. "You really want to talk about cardboard boxes right now?"

"Hell, no. Far better uses for our mouths."

He kissed her, a soft caress of his lips over hers. Returning a second time, nipping at her lower lip. Smiling as she sighed and softened under him, threading her fingers through his hair then dancing over his shoulders.

Familiar, not boring. Their sexual adventures might have changed over the past six years, but they hadn't gotten any less satisfying. He kissed her again, adjusting his thigh between her legs and rocking slightly.

Another sigh from her. A sudden gasp as he cupped her ass and lifted slightly, adding pressure to her core.

"You're dangerous, Caleb Stone."

"You're mine." The words came out more growly than he'd intended, but it was true, no matter what.

Tamara pressed a hand between them, rubbing the ridge of his cock. "Bed? Or right here?"

"Here." He shoved off her jeans in answer, dropping to his knees. Here at least to start.

The next minutes passed in a blur as Caleb enjoyed himself immensely. They moved from the wall to the floor, from the floor to the bed. Tamara softly cursed a few times, but mostly her noises let him know exactly what she was enjoying this go round by moaning or adjusting his fingers into a different position. She'd already had an orgasm before he took her from behind, curling his arms around her to keep their torsos tightly together until he lost his mind and Tamara shook under him.

Collapsing, he was thankful they'd made it to the bed.

Still panting, she rolled to face him, a wide grin in place as she stroked the hair off his forehead. "That was a nice afternoon surprise."

"For me, too," Caleb assured her. He watched her face, fascinated as always that he still had more to learn about her. More ways to show her how much she meant to him. "Seven months until Tyler starts school."

Her lips twitched. "I love that kiddo to pieces, but I also have a timer set in my head. No children around all day long? It's going to be a big adjustment."

"I'll do my best to help you pass the time," Caleb offered.

"Very generous. I look forward to taking you up on that." Tamara nodded slowly. "Every step of the way there have been things to enjoy. Raising the girls, having Tyler. Being your wife." She stroked his cheek. "Being your lover."

"You're more beautiful now than when I fell in love with you." Caleb caught her hand in his and kissed her knuckles. "I'm not only saying that because we just had sex, either."

She laughed. "I can honestly tell you that's one of the things I love about you. I have never had a doubt about how much you enjoy my body. But I know you enjoy my company, too, even when sex isn't on the table."

"Or the door, or the floor, or the—"

Tamara patted him on the chest. "Even those places. Turkey."

"I love you." He said it the way he tried to every single time. With his full concentration and his whole heart.

She touched their noses together and happy-sighed in his face. "Love you, too."

By the time they'd gotten dressed and headed back to the kitchen, Caleb was eyeing his watch. If they were lucky, they had maybe five minutes before the kids would be back in the house. "Need help with supper since I messed with your prep time?"

"Shoot. I forgot to tell you." Tamara picked up the box again and began taping the flaps open. "We're headed to Karen and Finn's for supper. Followed by some mischief-making."

"It wouldn't be a trip to one of your sister's without mischief. No problem." Caleb leaned on the island and watched Tamara tape bright red hearts to the edge of the box. She'd tell him more about what that was all about when she was ready. For now, another question was more important. "Is Jinx coming with us?"

Tamara paused. "I hadn't thought of asking, but there's no reason why she can't. It's not a bad idea. Karen won't mind, and Sasha would love it."

"Jinx is a good kid." Caleb hesitated, glancing out the window to make sure no one was about to step inside. "I'm glad Declan stopped by and told us what's going on over at the animal shelter, though. I had my suspicions it wasn't cut and dried, but I was leaning toward something more sinister."

"Me, too." Tamara paused, resting the box on the island. "The Skyes are good people, Caleb. Their hearts are in the right place, and they're trying to make a difference. I get it. Sometimes doing things a little sideways is what's needed."

Caleb examined her carefully. "You're thinking about the past. The news you shared with your friend even though it wasn't professionally allowed by the medical system."

Tamara answered slowly. "Not following the rules cost me, but in the end, one thing led to another and I'm exactly where I need to be." She closed the distance between them, laying a hand on his arm. "I lost my job in Rocky but found you and the girls. I found my *home*. So yeah, colouring outside the box doesn't bother me that much."

"Agreed." Outside, he could see the rest of the family

approaching. "Anything I need to do to get the horde ready to head to Karen's?"

"Oh, yes." Tamara picked up the box and wiggled it in the air. "We need to get ready for Boxy."

2

KAREN

The tip of Dandelion Fluff's tail quivered a second before the white cat pounced. Tyler's shriek of laughter echoed in the living room where Finn was entertaining the little guy with help from Dandy.

Her heart pounded in her throat as Karen turned half her attention on the action in the kitchen and half on the man she loved more than anything as he picked up his nephew and flipped Tyler upside down, the two of them laughing like hyenas.

Finn always has loved kids.

"Hey, Auntie Karen, we're ready for you."

Karen turned to smile at her oldest niece. "You sure about that, Sasha?"

"We figured out the lighting problem. Plus, Jinx and Sasha hung a blanket so we have a plain background." Tamara stepped away from the phone attached to the tripod, gesturing Karen into position. "If you do the honours, Caleb and I will people wrangle."

"Excellent. I'm all wrangled out after this week," Karen informed her sister.

"Lots of visitors?"

"For the last week of February, I expected a lull. Nope—we had seven out of eight cabins filled."

"Nice."

"Even nicer, they all went home this afternoon, happy and contented." Karen gestured to the box. "Take your places."

It was a fascinating idea. One at a time, starting with the girls, each person leaned over the table and poked their head through the box. Tamara helped adjust their hair or the props they held, while Caleb joined Karen and coordinated from there.

"Look up here," Caleb ordered Emma, lifting his hand above his head.

Emma's blonde curls bounced as she tilted her head and raised the wand she'd decided to hold. "Does it look as if I'm casting a spell?" she asked.

"Definitely," Karen said. "I can picture Petra photoshopping in a spark shooting from the tip of your wand."

"Perfect." Emma adjusted position a few times then gave up the box.

Each person had their own twist they wanted to add to the picture. Tyler wanted to ride the hobbyhorse Finn had made for him to play with at their house.

And he wanted to wear Caleb's cowboy hat.

"It's too big for you," Caleb told him gently.

"I know." Tyler jammed it on his head anyway and crawled into the box.

Caleb exchanged a glance with Tamara, who shrugged. "It's for fun, so why not?" she tossed back.

Karen barely kept from laughing as Tyler poked his head out, nothing but his mouth visible under his daddy's hat.

"Hey, Ty. Got an idea. Kneel on the table." She marched forward and rearranged the hobby horse so it looked as if it was exploding out of the box. "You might want to stay close in case things tip over," she told Tamara.

"Can do. I see what you're doing." Tamara tapped her son on the nose. "Lean out of the box, and I'll get that hat settled so we can see your smile."

In the end, it took a piece of rope and Caleb standing on the table so he could hold his son in mid-air, but the final picture had a happy Tyler riding his hobby horse right out of the box.

Sasha was easier—she rested her chin on her left fist and hung her right hand out of the box, fingers curled into a C. Her best friend, Jinx, did the opposite, so when they lined the pictures up next to each other, their hands formed a heart.

"That's cute," Karen said. She eyed Jinx for a moment before leaning past her niece and whispering in her ear, "Is there something going on with you two? Because you make a cute couple."

Sasha snorted. "Besties, that's all. I'm definitely into guys, and Jinx is not into anyone right now."

"Fair enough."

By the time Caleb and Tamara were done, and Karen and Finn had their turns, Karen's cheeks hurt from laughing so much.

"I'll clean up the pictures then send them to you guys for final approval. I figured we could send Petra two or three and she can use what works best," Karen offered.

"Sounds great." Tamara hugged her tight. "See you...next week? Girl's night out at my place. We're making perogies for everyone who wants them. Plus, relaxing and chatting, of course."

"I'll be there."

Multiple hugs and kisses followed from Sasha, Emma, and Tyler. Jinx gave a wave, then the whole group slipped out into the darkness of the March evening.

"The house is always shockingly quiet after your sisters and their entourages leave." Finn caught Karen by the hand and guided her into the living room. Instead of the two easy chairs that they usually used, he headed to the couch, sitting in the corner and taking her down beside him.

Exactly what she needed. Karen settled in, leaning her back against his chest so she could stare out at the lights twinkling on the temporarily empty guest cabins. "I kind of like the noise."

"We both do, but it's nice to say goodnight to them and get to have our own quiet place back." He brushed his lips against her temple. "You're really good at spending time with your sisters and then not spending time with them."

Which was maybe a strange comment, but she understood. "We love each other very much, but we also want to live our own lives."

"You manage it well," Finn said. "It's clear that you enjoy each other's company, but I don't see it as if it's out of control or something hanging over your head that you feel obligated to do. Like you didn't have to have Julia and Lisa here as well as Tamara's group."

"Adding in Julia and Lisa and everyone they own makes it a horde gathering. We save those for special occasions."

He laughed. "Like every *other* week."

Yeah, he was kind of right. Still... "The fact that Julia lives across the yard and works with me every day—I guess it's kind of the same as when I lived at home and Lisa was there." It really had never hit her before. "You know what? I have never really worked anywhere without having family around."

"That's pretty neat."

They sat quietly for a minute, but not in silence. The fire crackled, and from the spot where he'd curled up in the crook of her leg, Dandelion Fluff purred loudly enough he sounded like a miniature motor.

How exactly did she go about saying what she needed to tell him? Her news was big and important and yet so very ordinary.

Just tell him.

"Hey, Finn?"

Another soft kiss to her temple. "Yeah?"

The words slipped out. "I'm pregnant."

Behind her, every muscle in his body turned to stone. His hands on her shoulders tightened and he twisted her to face him.

His eyes flitted over her as if he couldn't believe his ears. "What did you say?"

Maybe she'd had no words before, but all of them spilled out now like the flood gates had opened. "I know when nothing was happening baby-wise, we did all those tests, and nothing conclusive showed up. And I know we had a conversation about how maybe it just wasn't meant to be. I mean, I'm thirty-seven—"

Finn's mouth hung open, but there was a far too serious look in his eyes for the miracle announcement she'd just shared. "I won't ask you if you're sure. But..."

"I'm sure. I've been waiting just in case, so I'm almost eight weeks along." She swallowed hard, brushing her fingers over the furrow that had appeared between his brows. "I wasn't trying to keep it secret, but I just didn't dare hope at the start. Then I felt like I needed to wait a little longer, but I feel good. Different—very different—but good."

"Oh my God." Finn wrapped his arms around her and pulled her close, holding her tight. He pressed her head to his chest, locking her in place. Under her ear, his heart was a horse galloping around the arena.

She got it. She'd had eight weeks to untangle it and still felt like it wasn't real. He was in the first moments of dealing with the entire mental change, and if he needed to hold her for the rest of the night, she would have understood.

When he finally let her up, he shook his head slightly. "Sorry if I screw this up. I'm excited but also scared to death."

Exactly what she was dealing with. "Trust me, I get it."

Finn caught her hands in his, linking their fingers together. "I'm going to trust that everything goes smoothly. I'm going to trust that you stay safe. But I also know I'm going to have nightmares."

"We can't do anything but hope right now," Karen pointed out.

"I'm hoping like crazy," Finn said. "But I'm worried, too. I don't want you to be hurt. Not physically, but not emotionally either. I know how hard it's been. When things weren't happening."

Karen nodded slowly. "When we didn't think we could have kids, we said that we'd be okay. Sad, but okay. That you and I were enough, and that's still true. If everything goes well, we'll welcome another family member into our lives and do everything we can to enjoy every minute of it." She took a deep breath. "And if it still ends up that it's just you and me, we *will* be enough. I mean that. I love you so much."

"So just take it one day at a time?" Finn eyed her. "And see a doctor ASAP..."

"Yes." She nodded decisively. "We'll make an appointment tomorrow. I know we're still going to hold our breaths for a few weeks until we're...sure."

"But we'll do it together," Finn promised. He leaned in and kissed her tenderly. "I'm so excited."

"Me too." No matter how big her happiness inside was, it still came out a whisper.

And that was okay. Sometimes hope and excitement were a quiet wind blowing on a cold, moonlit night.

3

PETRA

*P*ictures were piling up nicely in her file marked WEDDING IN A BOX. She'd wanted to wait until there were enough to get an idea of how best to place the lot, but with a couple dozen photos available to play with, Petra couldn't wait any longer.

Sunshine poured in the window of her and Aiden's apartment, so she twisted the computer to a better angle on the kitchen table. Then she rubbed her hands together with glee, cackled loudly, and dove in.

Minutes later, a firm hand landed on her shoulder. "*Petra.*"

"Huh?" She glanced up and blinked hard. "Hey. What's up?"

"I've called your name five times," Aiden teased. "You're far too focused."

She wiggled in her seat, swearing when she checked the clock. "Is that really the time?"

"Yes."

Drat. She'd been at it for two hours. "Oops. I'm late for supper."

He leaned over her shoulder, admiring the screen. "Tansy said to come find you, so you're not in the naughty corner—yet. Those look amazing."

"Isn't it fun?" Petra moved the mouse and adjusted the screen size so he could see the entire image at once. "We've already gotten so many photos that I've decided we'll need more than one collage. Good thing we took a bunch of shots of us to use as centerpieces with the rest of our friends framing us."

"Well, it is our wedding, so us in the starring position is acceptable." Aiden poked his nose closer to her computer. "Is that...a fairy?"

Petra snorted. "Cupid. Madison, whom I know from Girls' Night Out—her husband is Ryan from Rough Cut—their littlest is six months old. I have no idea how they made that kid wings, but Mikayla looks adorable."

"Adorable, yes, but why is she aiming her arrow at Cody Gabrielle from Red Boot ranch?"

Petra did a double take. "She's shooting at us."

"Ahh." He shrugged. "I'm already well and truly speared by love's arrow. She can shoot Cody if she wants."

A laugh escaped. "People were so creative. My oldest sister dressed the entire family in bright yellow with pink accents. They nearly glow, they're so bright."

Aiden twisted her chair to face him then tugged her to her feet and into his arms. "After supper, I want to see all the pictures. It's going to be a fantastic memory for us to look back on over the years."

"Putting this together makes it feel as if they were a part of our wedding." Petra eased into full hug mode, loving how perfect it was to be there with him. "They all look so happy for us."

"As they should." Aiden lifted her chin. "We might not do

everything by the book, but we do this part right. We both have family and friends who are rock solid. I'm glad, and I look forward to enjoying their company in the years to come."

"Bright yellow shirts, misaimed arrows, goats, and all," Petra offered.

Aiden's happy expression instantly folded into concern. "*Goats?*"

"Uh-huh."

He made a face. "Do I want to know?"

She snickered. "Don't worry. They look very festive."

His laughter vanished under the kiss she gave him.

IF YOU'D LIKE to find out more about that Cupid's bow aimed at Cody Gabrielle, **Fern's Date with Destiny** is the final novella in the Heart Falls Vignette and Novella series.

THE START OF US

In this trip back in time, we visit the beginning of the relationship between Ginny and Tucker.

Every February, Tucker returns to Heart Falls to honour the saddest day with his friends. They've shared good memories, and painful ones. This year, Tucker is trying his damnedest to not notice that his best friend's little sister is definitely all grown up. Not the place. Not the time.

Except Ginny thinks it's *definitely* the time, *and* the place, and there's not much use in arguing with a Stone.

Featuring: The Stone family: Caleb, Luke, Walker, Ginny, Darilyn Hayes (foster sister), Dustin, Tucker Stewart.

. . .

Timeline: This scene is set mostly in February, five years after tragedy struck the Silver Stone ranch, and five years before the Stones of Heart Falls series begins.

1

____

*E*very year after the accident, Tucker returned to Silver Stone ranch in February. Not that the Stone family held an official memorial or anything, but it seemed the right thing to do.

Caleb usually said something at the breakfast table and arranged to take his siblings up to their parents' hillside graves if the weather wasn't too miserable.

The first year the most noticeable change was that Caleb had a wife. Her presence wasn't a shock—Tucker had heard from Luke about Caleb's whirlwind courtship, but now here Wendy was, blonde, beautiful, and icy as hell.

Tucker kept his mouth shut, though, because it wasn't really his business. Besides, the woman had looked nearly ready to pop any minute, her baby belly overwhelmingly huge on her petite frame. There was no mistaking it—she and Caleb were solidly a unit.

A couple of years later when Tucker visited, Ginny and Dare hauled out photo albums from somewhere, which was both a huge hit and a terrible disaster. Tears flowed like spring rain even as the walls rang with laughter. It had been a celebration of life as much as a lament for their losses.

At this point, little Sasha was nearly three years old and had peeked at the pictures of the gramma and grandpa she'd never met with moderate interest before wandering away. Her little sister, Emma, a crawling toddler with blonde curls and endless energy, had settled in her Auntie Ginny's lap and tunelessly sang nonsense songs. Wendy still constantly looked as if she smelled something unpleasant, but she was relatively easy to ignore.

Ginny, nearly eighteen, had filled out in ways Tucker tried very hard not to notice. Long legs and sweet curves and...

He headed home a couple days early to avoid thinking too hard about all *those* changes.

But this year, five years after the accident, something felt different.

The room was heavy with unspoken grief during the evening meal, the limited conversation mostly fueled by fourteen year old Dusty, who seemed the most settled into the reality of his big brother and the rest of his siblings raising him.

Ginny and Dare took off as fast as possible once the meal was done. "Ginny's with me in the cottage tonight," Dare announced.

"Don't be late for chores in the morning," Caleb grumbled. But he hauled them both in for big hugs before silently letting them go.

Everyone grieves in their own way, Tucker figured.

"Come on," Luke demanded of Tucker. "We've got plans tonight as well."

"Don't you be late, either," Caleb warned.

"Always on time, big brother," Luke sang before grinning at

Walker, who'd drawn the short straw and was on wash-up duty that night. "Have fun with your dishpan hands."

Walker glanced around the room to see where the kids and Wendy were then rapidly flashed his middle finger.

Laughing, Luke hauled Tucker off to the barn for a little manly therapy, aka, beating the hell out of each other for a while.

A shot of excitement hit in spite of the sadness of the day. Fighting was outlawed in Tucker's home. The physical kind and the verbal, both being far too uncouth and undignified for his parents to endure. Even though at twenty-four Tucker now worked and roomed at a boarding stable away from his childhood home, the rules had been very thoroughly trained into him.

Luke stripped off his shirt then raised his fists, already weaving slightly as if he expected Tucker to attack without warning. "Ready?"

Whatever his friend needed, Tucker would offer. He'd take what he needed at the same time.

He jerked his shirt forward over his head. "You really want to do this? I don't want to mess up your pretty face before Friday night."

"Aim low, then."

Luke darted forward, jabbing hard at Tucker's ribs. He got in half a blow before Tucker pivoted to the side and swung. His knuckles thudded into Luke's chest.

Luke grabbed for him and tried to wrestle him to the ground.

"You're just asking to be embarrassed," Tucker drawled. He caught Luke around his torso and lifted his friend off his feet. Luke twisted far enough that Tucker lost his balance, and they both fell to the dirt floor.

Fighting was cathartic and, in a strange way, calming. An hour later, they were both sweaty and scuffed up, but Luke wore a grin and Tucker felt as if he were the king of the world.

"God, your fists are like rocks," Luke complained, stretching out his legs as he sucked back water. His chest rocked with sharp inhalations as he fought to catch his breath.

"Your ribs are dangerous," Tucker said dryly, settling onto a stool. "For a minute I thought I was going to get a hangnail."

"Jerk."

"Ass."

Luke grinned at him. Then his expression fell. "I'm glad you're here. Today sucks."

Sadness welled up in Tucker's belly. "It doesn't get much easier, does it?"

His friend stared at the wall for a silent minute before speaking softly. "Parts do. Sometimes I go whole weeks without thinking 'I need to let Dad know about—*whatever*.' Yet every time it happens, it slices so hard it's as if I just lost them."

He cut off, his voice thick with sorrow.

Tucker bowed his head, letting the pressure in his throat and chest wash over him. He breathed deep then lifted his gaze to his friend's. "Good."

Luke's brow furrowed, and his expression slid to confused.

"If it didn't hurt, you'd be angry at yourself," Tucker said quietly. "I know you. You've got a huge heart—it's okay that it still aches."

Luke nodded slowly. "Thanks. I needed to hear that." He hesitated then offered a grimace. "This is on the down-low. Don't tell anyone, okay?"

Tucker raised a brow at the other man. "Really? Do I need to pinkie swear that I'll keep your secret?"

"It's not my secret," Luke said. "I overheard Wendy telling

Caleb he was being ridiculous. That he was sentimental and stupid to try to hold onto the ranch."

"Shit." Tucker's opinion of the woman hadn't improved over time. He considered. "You think Caleb wants to sell the place?"

"Hell no, but *wants to* and *needs to* are different things, know what I mean?" Luke shook his head. "Wendy is not my favourite person."

"Mine either," Tucker agreed. "Be glad you don't have to live with her."

"Amen. I feel for Ginny, I really do." Luke made a face. "Even living in the basement of the ranch house means too much exposure to Wendy's negativity."

"She could move out to the bunkhouse..." Tucker stopped himself, the image of the curvy brunette surrounded by the ranch hands of Silver Stone doing something terrible to his gut.

He trusted them to have her back, but what if...

He met Luke's smirk. His friend snickered. "Yeah, that didn't take you long."

"Move in with Dare in the cottage?"

"I suggested that, but Ginny says she's staying put because Dusty and the little girls are still in the house. Plus someone needs to keep things rolling around the place since we all know Wendy is mostly useless."

It was hard to see his friends suffering, but it wasn't as if Tucker could give Caleb marriage advice. His parents were no shining example of how a marriage should work.

That had been the Stones and the Hayeses. People gone far too soon who had left a lasting memory.

Luke's phone went off. He glanced at the screen and his expression folded into a frown as he answered. "Ginny?"

Tucker couldn't hear her words, but Luke's reaction said enough.

He took a sharp breath. "Fuck. Stay put, and keep Dare there. I'll be out as quick as I can." Luke hung up and met Tucker's gaze. "They're not at the cottage like we thought, watching movies and crying. They're at the pub, and Dare is three sheets to the wind. Ginny can't get her to stop."

2

———

G inny Stone was all for people taking charge and going after what they needed. Especially her best friend, Dare, who more than deserved to be a little wild and outrageous if it soothed the demons that rode her every February tenth.

Okay, Ginny also had demons on this anniversary day, but she'd had her brothers to turn to. Dare had lost everyone.

But the night was not going as planned.

They hadn't set out to do anything illegal, and hoped to stay on the correct side of immoral, but now the aforementioned *wild and outrageous* from Dare was tilting hard toward trouble.

Which was to say Dare wasn't up on the bar dancing. Yet.

It had started simply. They were both old enough to be in the pub, even though the owner and bartender, Rex Matter, had given them both the evil eye for a few minutes.

Did he think they were simply going to dance and not drink? What did it matter? The more ladies out on the floor, the greater the chances some of the cowboys would stick around in the hopes of a dance, drinking as they waited.

Ginny slid up to the bar, hauled there by Dare, and once again wondered if Rex had been on the receiving end of a series of lectures to *watch out for my sisters or else* from the Stone patriarchy.

"Evening, Rex," Ginny said with a bright smile.

Rex didn't pause in drying the glass in his hands but dipped his chin politely. "Ladies. Your brothers lurking nearby?"

Ginny forced the smile to stick. "Just us. We'd like to start a tab."

He eyed them before bestowing another nod. "What'll it be tonight? Iced tea? Pop?"

"Whiskey." The word shot out of Dare like a warning shot across a ship's bow. Quick, with attitude.

Ginny didn't blame her friend. The bartender had seemed one step away from suggesting Shirley Temples.

Rex raised a brow, meeting Ginny's gaze. "You?"

"The same." Although whiskey wasn't her favourite, she'd do one shot then redirect the party in a safer direction. For the sake of her pocketbook if nothing else.

Dare waited until they both held tumblers of the amber liquid before raising hers in the air toward Ginny. "Tonight we toast our families. Starting with your mom."

Oh God. Ginny's throat tightened.

Her friend's gaze locked on hers. "She always told us to *do the next thing.* I remembered that so often in the days after the accident when I wasn't sure how to get out of bed. I still wake up thinking it at times."

Memories threatened to take Ginny out at the knees. Deb Stone offering that all-knowing smile to the girls as they tried to jump ahead faster than they should. "One step at a time," Ginny gave back to Dare.

They clinked glasses, then Dare upended hers. The liquid seemed to vanish from sight, and suddenly the tumbler was on the counter and Dare was looking at her expectantly.

Ginny lifted the glass and sipped.

Fire rolled over her tongue and down her throat, but the burn was good and eased the hurt of memory. Still, she took her time, making a face at Dare when her friend crossed her arms over her chest.

"You plan on being like this all night?" Dare demanded.

"You plan on being like this all night?" Ginny offered back with a wink as she took another sip.

Dare's eye roll was epic, but she tilted her head toward the side of the room where a high-top had just opened up. "Get us two more. I'll nab the table."

Which gave Ginny the opportunity to put her remaining finger of whiskey down on the nearest table before heading back to the bar.

"Another round, please, Rex." Ginny debated. "Can you put ice in them this time?"

He nodded then moved without further comment, the lineup of people waiting for their drinks growing busy enough to make him not interrogate her.

Ginny accepted the drinks he pushed across the bar then glanced toward the high-top.

Dare offered the tall cowboy leaning against the support post beside her a polite smile—one that didn't even try to touch her eyes. Her ass stayed firmly planted on her stool, not budging an inch.

Ginny took advantage of the distraction, quickly tipping half of each drink into an abandoned glass on a side table.

Here's hoping Dare wouldn't notice the huge drop in alcohol this go-round.

Ginny marched over to her friend, depositing the glasses on the tabletop. "Noisy tonight."

"Great music, though." The cowboy's gaze drifted from Dare to Ginny, his expression brightening with a little too much confidence. "Hey, sweet curves," he said, smiling. "Want to dance?"

Ginny didn't bother smiling. She waved a hand between them, gesturing to her admittedly ample chest, then up to her face. "My eyes are up here, *hoss*."

Dare snorted, clearly used to Ginny taking the lead when things got awkward. "Mattias here says he's an excellent dancer," she said, tone dry as dust.

Dancing was a viable out from the drinking, but not with this fine example of manhood. Ginny had a strict *one strike, and you're out* policy. "Fantastic," Ginny said. "But Dare and I have plans tonight that don't involve entertaining cowboys."

"Just you two, eh?" His smirk widened. "I'd love to watch."

The braying laugh that escaped Ginny was far from attractive, but the suddenness of it made him lean back far enough that when she picked up her stool and swung it to a new position closer to Dare, the legs only grazed Mattias's shins.

He cursed and straightened, the sleaze vanishing as his expression turned ugly. "Goddamn cock teases."

The small group of men at the table to their right froze instantly, tension radiating from them like a beacon. Two of them slid off their stools and rose to form a barrier between the unwanted cowboy and Dare and Ginny.

"You want to move along," one of the deep-voiced men suggested.

Mattias sized up the situation then smartly beat a hasty retreat.

The table was full of Silver Stone ranch hands. Paul, one of the older men who'd been around for long enough to work for their fathers, turned to Ginny.

"Pleasant sort," he offered mildly.

She snorted. "Thanks for the intercept. Sorry to interrupt your night."

"No problem." He considered for a moment. "You gals want company?"

"Love some," Dare offered instantly. "Only Ginny and I have a toast to make every now and then. If that's okay with you."

"You call 'em," Paul returned. He tilted his head toward his table. "Grab the open chairs. We'll find more if we need them. Most of the guys are up and down dancing anyway."

Dare flashed him a thumbs up then picked up her new glass and eyed it suspiciously before giving Ginny the stink eye. "Whiskey *neat*, you jerk."

"Whatever." Ginny took control and raised her glass. "To your mom. Who made the inside of your cabin feel like it was a palace, a cozy retreat, and always, always a home."

Tears shone in Dare's eyes as they clinked glasses. "To Mom."

The ice had partially melted, making it easier to drink the shot in one go. They both put down their empties, then Ginny was enveloped in a tight, needy hug.

She squeezed her friend back just as intensely.

"I miss her." Dare's words came out shaky.

"I know," Ginny offered.

When they pulled apart, Ginny was hopeful the evening was back on track. Sad, but a way to deal with enough emotional baggage to create their own personal Mount Everest.

Sitting with the Silver Stone crew meant they were safe, and Ginny relaxed a touch. The table was covered with a layer of empty beer bottles and glasses, making it easier for her to discard most of the new drinks after a single sip without Dare noticing.

And there were new drinks. The next two times, Dare asked a different ranch hand to grab them their drinks. The tab was still under Dare's name, but it meant whiskeys arrived every ten minutes or so.

"Wait," Ginny interrupted after the fourth shot, desperate to regain control. "We need something special this time."

Dare raised a brow.

It wasn't only an attempt to slow her friend down. Inspiration hit, and with it, tears nearly burst free. "We need a drink in honour of Shayla."

Dare's little sister who had also lost her life in the accident. So young, so much future in front of her, gone—

Across from Ginny, Dare's lips quivered. Then she nodded, hard. "I'm getting these for us."

She rose from the table and headed for the bar like a bull on a mission. A slightly tipsy bull, considering the crooked path she wove.

"Ginny." Paul leaned into her right shoulder. "You doing okay?"

"Mostly. It's a tough day," Ginny admitted.

He nodded his understanding. "Your daddy was a good man. I'm sorry he's gone." He cleared his throat. "I'm heading out in about half an hour because I have a shift at four a.m. Some of the others will stay for a bit, but are you two going to be all right?"

"Absolutely," Ginny insisted. "You're not expected to babysit us. Although I do appreciate the save earlier."

"You would have hit him with your purse if he'd taken half a step forward," Paul drawled. "Yeah?"

She patted her bag, enjoying the reassuring heavy weight of it. "I have a brick in here."

He laughed before eyeing her closer. "You're not drinking. Not really, are you?"

She shook her head. "I'm clear headed and in control. I have family on speed dial. So you go ahead and enjoy the rest of your evening."

He tipped his hat then moved back to the lively discussion on the far side of the table.

Dare reappeared, tall drinks in her hands and a grin on her slightly inebriated face. "For Shayla. She would have adored these."

The drink presented to Ginny was a Shirley Temple. "I bet Rex was over the moon."

Dare snorted as she sat. "He liked the drink order, not the *special* order."

She pointed, so Ginny took a closer look.

The drink was tall and very pink. The skewer across the top held three maraschino cherries, glowing in that classic, over-the-top, unearthly red. Like ticking sugar bombs waiting to explode.

Ginny reached for her glass and hoped her liver was up to the food colouring overload.

3

<hr>

Rough Cut looked like it always did—dim lighting, sticky floor, walls that hadn't seen new paint since before cell phones were a thing. Still, it was familiar, and most nights, welcoming.

Tonight the energy inside ricochetted like a raccoon caught in a karaoke machine.

Tucker stepped through the door behind Luke and immediately winced at the off-key wailing coming from center floor.

"God help us," he muttered.

On the tiny dance area, Dare twirled wildly, her long limbs flying, her hips a beat ahead of the music as she butchered the lyrics to a country ballad. It might've hit harder if it weren't screeched at double volume and punctuated by jazz hands. The only line Tucker caught was something like *"I ain't your angel, and you sure ain't mine..."*

"'Angel of the Broken Heart'?" Luke guessed beside him. "That's gotta be it. Poor Reba's rolling in her grave, and she's not even dead."

Dare had clearly tried to make a dramatic fashion statement—her jacket half-off, a second shirt tied around her waist, hair tousled as if she'd fought someone to keep her boots.

And Ginny, poor Ginny, clung to her side like a human seatbelt.

She didn't look drunk—more like exhausted and deeply, profoundly over it.

"Okay," Luke said grimly. "Time to go."

Rex, the bartender, nodded at them with his usual stiff-jawed disapproval, then he shocked the hell out of Tucker by calling out gruffly, "I'll cover their tab. Just get that one home."

Tucker gave the man a quick salute. "Thanks."

Ahead of him, Luke wove through the crowd with the kind of single-minded determination usually reserved for men facing down a raging bull. He reached Dare just as she flung her arms wide for a dramatic spin, and he caught her mid-revolution.

"Whoa there, Patsy," Luke said, scooping her off the floor like a rogue pageant contestant having a breakdown. "Time to exit stage left."

Dare blinked at him then patted his cheek affectionately. "Awww. You're the bestest big brother. You came."

"Yep." He adjusted her in his arms as she sagged against him, the emotional energy suddenly draining out of her. "You're done."

Ginny sagged too—but only in relief. She turned toward Tucker, breath hitching, her expression pinched with gratitude and mortification in equal parts.

"She wouldn't leave." Ginny's voice was tight. "I didn't know what else to do."

"You did good," Tucker said quietly, resting a hand on the small of her back. "We've got her."

As Luke carried Dare toward the door, Ginny followed. Tucker stepped beside her, instinctively slipping an arm around her shoulders when she swayed a little too far to the left.

She immediately stiffened. "I'm not drunk."

"Didn't say you were."

"You don't need to carry me."

"I'm not."

"You're carrying me with your arm."

"That's not how carrying works." He eased it away but didn't quite step back. "I'm walking beside you, Stone. You'd know if I carried you."

Ginny shot him a look. "Would I?"

Something zinged low in Tucker's gut at the mental image of her cradled in his arms, but he tamped it down fast. Tonight was not the night.

"Come on," he said, holding the door for her. "Let's get Dare home before she decides to go for round three of the talent show."

The instant the truck doors were unlocked, Luke climbed into the back seat, settling Dare on his lap like a sack of half-drunken potatoes. She leaned against him, humming tunelessly into his neck.

Which left Ginny the front passenger seat, her arms wrapped tightly across her chest as she angled her body toward the door.

Tucker pulled out of the gravel lot, headlights sweeping across a cow statue with a Santa hat hanging from one horn.

February in Alberta. Yeehaw.

Tucker winced as Dare's humming morphed back into full volume wailing again. He thought it might have been "You Were Mine" by the Chicks, but she kept sliding into what sounded suspiciously like early Carrie Underwood.

Ginny groaned and let her head drop back onto the seat,

exhaling like it hurt. "I think that's the third key change in this verse."

Luke chuckled dryly from the back. "She's got spirit."

"She's got whiskey," Ginny muttered.

Luke tried to redirect Dare with a quieter tune, humming "Cowboy Take Me Away" in her ear like a lullaby. It worked—sort of. At least she stopped belting out half coherent lyrics.

"Want to tell me how it got this far?" Tucker asked quietly.

Ginny rubbed her face then dropped her hands to her lap. "She wanted to toast the people we lost. All of them. So one drink each for our parents, then for hers and Shayla."

Tucker winced. "That's five drinks."

"Shayla's was non-alcoholic, thank God. But then Dare got sentimental. Decided she had a new family now who all needed to be appreciated. Her boys. That was five. Then her new sister —me." Ginny blinked hard, glancing out the window. "Six."

Tucker gave a low whistle. "Please don't say she got to seven."

"Oh, she did." Ginny huffed a laugh. "A toast to 'whoever the hell ends up being her future family, poor bastards who will have to deal with her.' Her words."

"I don't know if that's touching or terrifying," Tucker said.

"Both."

They lapsed into silence as the ranch turnoff came into view. He flicked on the signal even though no one else was on the road.

Snow crunched under the tires as he rolled north, past the main ranch house and toward Dare's cabin. The cabin glowed welcomingly, the golden pool of porch light reaching fingers into the February darkness that had fallen hours ago.

Tucker parked at the base of the four steps leading to the deck.

"I've got her," Luke murmured, shifting Dare in his arms and easing out the door. "She's mostly dead weight now."

Dare perked up just enough to say, "I resent that," before she leaned over and vomited onto the snow covered grass.

Ginny winced but jumped out to help. She was at Dare's side a second later, rubbing her back and murmuring softly.

Together, the three of them managed to get Dare up the steps and inside the cottage. Tucker hurried ahead far enough to get the door open and spot the soft glow of the kitchen light.

The place was exactly as he remembered—two bedrooms, warm with wood paneling, the faint scent of cinnamon on the air. One room held a double bed and dark curtains. The other had a desk with two computer monitors and a narrow single bed pushed up against the wall. A cozy blend of past and present.

"I'll stay with her tonight," Luke said firmly as they guided Dare into her room. "She'll need someone here if she wakes up."

"I can do that—" Ginny began, but Luke cut her off.

He turned to her with a gentler tone. "You need a break. Help get Dare into pajamas, then I'll handle the rest. You did everything you could, Gin. Let it go."

Ginny nodded, her lips pressed tight.

She guided Dare down to the bathroom, and the water ran briefly as Dare alternated between brushing her teeth and singing a dirge.

Luke caught Tucker's gaze. "You'll get Ginny home?"

"Of course." Tucker pressed a hand to his friend's shoulder. "You okay?"

"Just pissed, like usual, that life handed us such a shitty hand." Luke glanced toward the bathroom. "Do I wish she hadn't gotten trashed? Absolutely. But hell if I'm going to tell her that she was wrong. Anything that makes the pain better for today is understandable."

Erasing the pain. What Tucker wouldn't do to make that a reality for any of his friends.

A moment later, Ginny popped out of the primary bedroom, speaking softly through the open door. "I love you, Dare."

"Luv ya, Truth," Dare slurred back.

Ginny paused to hug her brother. "Thanks for coming to get us."

"I'd say any time, but you know what I mean."

She snorted softly. "Yeah."

Tucker followed Ginny back outside, the porch light a warm glow above them. She stepped down the stairs but paused halfway to the truck.

"I don't want to go back to the ranch," she said quietly.

Tucker frowned. "You worried about Caleb?"

She shook her head. "He'd probably understand. But Wendy…" Her voice trailed off, and she let out a hard sigh. "She'll find some way to make this all my fault. She'll twist tonight into something ugly. Uglier."

Tucker felt that like a punch. He'd seen how Wendy treated Ginny—polite, sharp-edged, dismissive. Passive-aggressive turned straight-up aggressive at times—out of Caleb's hearing though.

"I'll take you anywhere you want," he said. "Main house is out, obviously. Dare's place is full. Bunkhouse?"

"Full of hands." Ginny looked up at him, hair windblown, cheeks flushed with cold and frustration. "What about your place?"

"My—" She'd lost him.

"You've got the horse trailer." She lifted one shoulder. "It's got heat. A door. Privacy."

Temptation hit like a truck.

She didn't mean anything by it—he knew that. She wanted safety. Comfort. Not him. Not like that.

But the thought of her within arm's reach, curled up in that little bunk behind the tack wall—

Tucker swallowed hard. "Yeah," he said hoarsely. "Yeah, that'll work."

God help him.

4

———

She had never been so exhausted and so full of want at the same time.

Tucker's horse trailer-turned-temporary-residence was warm, dimly lit, and smelled faintly of leather and hay. He offered her the narrow bunk against the wall while he took the saddle bench, like some kind of gentleman outlaw from an old western who still knew his manners.

Ginny kicked off her boots and climbed up without waiting for permission, folding her knees under her and wrapping herself in the thick throw blanket.

"You ready for bed?" he asked.

"Wired. It's only eight p.m." She shook her head. "That was way too much mischief in way too short a time."

He eyed her. "Need some Tylenol? Get ahead of the drink headache?"

"I had a total of maybe two drinks, watered down, plus the equivalent of a cup of sugar laced with red dye number three." She shuddered. When he cringed as well, Ginny laughed.

"Yeah, I might never be able to look a maraschino in the eye again."

"You have to admit Dare is creative. Which we all knew with her blogging and all that." Tucker pulled out a deck of cards and held them up. "Want to pass the time for a bit while you come down off the adrenaline high?"

"May as well."

How she managed not to suggest strip poker as a great starting point—sainthood waited for her, right around the corner.

The wind rattled the trailer's aluminum skin. It was only February, so winter had a long time to hang on. The night smelled more like thawing mud than snow, with a Chinook wind blowing from the west, but in Alberta, thinking of spring now was more than a fool's game, it was downright wrong.

She watched Tucker's hands as he shuffled. Strong. Familiar.

And hers, if she could just get him to admit it.

"You were a good friend to Dare tonight," he said finally, passing her the cards and going to the small fridge to grab them drinks.

Ginny exhaled softly. "I tried."

"You succeeded." He brought back two cans of ginger ale and offered her one.

"She's the strongest person I know, but sometimes even that strength turns in on her." Ginny shrugged. "She misses them. Her sister, her parents. The hurt just sneaks up."

Tucker nodded, slow and thoughtful. "And you were the only one who could keep her steady until we got there."

Ginny snorted. "That was me keeping her steady? You missed the part where she tried to strip off her tank top to make a 'sacrifice to the whiskey gods.' I stopped her by bribing her with more cherries."

A grin tugged at the corner of his mouth. "Smart. Effective."

Ginny smiled but didn't look away. "I'm serious. Thank you. For coming tonight. For helping her. For helping me."

Tucker glanced up, and something in his eyes flashed that looked like regret. "You don't have to thank me. You're family."

Family.

She let the word sit between them. Not out of bitterness— she knew what he meant. But God, if only he knew what *she* meant.

"I'm not a kid anymore," she said, quiet but sure. "I'm all grown up."

Tucker raised a brow, his gaze flicking up and down in a deliberately light-hearted gesture. "No argument from me."

"Don't look at me like that," she snapped, patience wearing thin.

"Like what?"

"With lying eyes."

Tucker blinked in surprise. "What's *that* mean?"

"That you're totally looking and like what you see but pretending that you're not. Probably because I'm Luke's little sister or something equally stupid, but you *have* noticed that I'm not twelve anymore."

He shrugged and picked up the cards again.

"You're not going to admit it? That you're interested? That *we're* interested in...more."

Tucker determinedly shuffled the cards, not meeting her eyes.

"*Tucker.*" This time she said it softly. Yearning and yet somehow unable to straight out say it. *I want you. I've wanted you forever.*

The expression on his face as he cautiously glanced up said he'd heard it. The said *and* the unsaid. The drift of his eyes over her torso burned as clearly as if he'd dragged a finger over her, heat smoldering just under her skin.

A second later, it was as if he'd been poked with a cattle prod. He stiffened, and an unnatural smile replaced the smolder.

The pretending version of Tucker turned cocky. One of his brows winged upward. "Ready to play?"

Asshole. She knew this thing between them was complicated, but still, she didn't deserve to be lied to, not like this. "I hope my boobs burned your retinas."

He snorted, which made at least some of the real Tucker return to his eyes.

Fine, Ginny needed some time to cool off. She'd give him a break for a short while, but before the night was out, she planned to give the stubborn bastard a run for the stubborn championship. She wanted every trace of liquor gone from her system so that couldn't be his excuse to shut her down.

They played endless rounds of gin rummy.

Tucker told her about the place he was working. Rich horse owners who were alternatively snooty and needy as they brought in under-exercised rides and suddenly realized they needed the hired help. Ginny told him about the garden and greenhouse Caleb had agreed to build, and her hopes to get a community supported agriculture garden box off the ground the following spring.

"You've always loved the garden," he said. "And your herbs. The teas you make are great. Except for *the one*."

She was never going to live that down. "Luke is none the worse for a little food poisoning."

"You might have improved him." Tucker was grinning again.

An hour passed. Another. Comfortable and familiar.

Maddening.

They'd been sitting there since just past eight, the trailer slowly getting warmer and warmer around them. Or maybe that was just Ginny's libido kicking into overdrive. The compact space meant every time he moved, or she did, something connected.

He stripped off a layer, and she had to concentrate to stop from staring at his forearms. She pulled off her flannel shirt, and his gaze drifted from his hand of cards to her breasts and then back to his cards with an iron will.

Yeah, she had his number. Breast man, all the way.

Finally, it was nearly eleven o'clock. She deliberately put the playing cards aside then stretched out her legs.

She didn't pull them back when her toes brushed his thigh.

He wiggled briefly but didn't jerk away.

Time. It was *past* time.

"You remember the summer Luke dated Courtney Masseny?" she asked.

Tucker's smile faltered, just a little. "I remember." He made a face. "That relationship was thankfully short lived."

She snorted. "Agreed. But as a side note, I had a wicked crush on you that summer."

Tucker blinked. "What?"

Amusement rose. "What, you didn't hear me, or what, you can't believe it?"

"My brain isn't registering the comment properly." His expression made that clear. He'd truly had no idea. "If I do the math right, you were fourteen. You liked to eat Pop-Tarts with pickles."

"And I dreamed of kissing you behind the barn," she confessed. "Which was about as far as my teenage brain dared to go back then. Kissing. So scandalous."

Silence.

"I think my mom knew." Ginny's cheeks flamed, but the

truth was the truth, and that's what she was known for sharing. "*She's* the reason you didn't have to deal with an infatuated teenager following you around the ranch all day and night for the next year."

His entire body stilled.

Ginny leaned forward, resting her elbows on her knees. "I left you alone because Mom was right—you needed your time with Luke, and I needed time to grow up. But the truth is the way I felt never changed."

He opened his mouth.

She held up a hand. "Let me finish."

He nodded.

"I get it. The timing for me to say something has always been tricky. Life got messy with the accident. You were Luke's best friend. I was too young. You're always careful. And I appreciate that. But I'm not too young anymore, and I'm not confused about what I want."

"Ginny—"

"This is what I want. You. This night. Us." Her voice shook just a little, but she steadied it with another breath. "I would never have wished for Dare to end up mindlessly drunk on the anniversary of losing her whole world, but I can't pretend I'm not grateful for what created a moment alone with you."

Tucker was frozen.

"Today is awful. Mom and Dad are gone forever. Caleb and Luke— Hell, you know what we've all had to deal with for the last five years. You've been here. You've helped." She slipped her hand over his. "If something good could happen—on this day of all days—maybe it won't always be just pain and bad memories."

He stared at her for long enough that the wind outside seemed to still.

Then his whole expression shifted. The warmth of family and friendship was replaced by something fierce. Intense.

His lips parted slightly, a muscle ticking in his jaw. That was his tell—his heart was racing. He was thinking too hard and too fast and didn't know where to put any of it.

Ginny sat very still. For once in her life, she didn't press further. Didn't push. She'd said what she came to say.

Now it was his turn.

5

---

*T*ucker had thought a lot of things about this day in February over the years. That it was cursed. That it was a weight he'd carry forever. That it was cruel to keep expecting any kind of light to shine through something so heavy.

He had not expected it to feel like this—his chest so full of hope and heat he could hardly breathe.

Ginny sat across from him, her face open and brave. Every word she'd spoken echoed like a bell in his ribs. *This is what I want. You. This night. Us.*

He was already halfway gone.

"Ginny," he said quietly. "I hear you. I do. But if we take tonight, I don't want it to end in hurting you worse."

Her lips quirked. "Because you're not living here? Not able to be my full-time boyfriend?"

He opened his mouth to explain, but she beat him to it.

"I'm not looking for promises of forever. I'm looking for warm hands and hot kisses and to be able to turn my brain off for one goddamned minute this day and think about— *No. Not* to *think* at all because you've got me so off-kilter all I can do is feel."

Tucker's heart kicked once, hard enough it felt like a warning. But it sure as hell didn't stop him.

"Are you going to tell Dare?" he asked. "Am I supposed to tell Luke?"

Ginny's eyes softened, but the heat in them never wavered. "That's up to you. But I'd suggest we're adults. What we do is our business and no one else's." Then a wicked sparkle danced across her face. "Also, Luke will beat you up. I don't want that on my conscience."

Tucker huffed. "He'd try."

Their smiles met and held, full of history and something new stirring just beneath it. It was right—laughter and anticipation, sexual tension braided with friendship.

"I'd tell Dare someday," Ginny said, voice quieter now. "But not tonight or any time soon. Tonight is for us. Here and now."

He stood and offered her his hand. "Then here and now starts with this."

She took it without hesitation.

Tucker helped her off the bunk and pulled her to him, slow and sure. Her body settled against his as if it was always meant to. He lifted his hand to her cheek, brushing a thumb along her jaw before he bent and kissed her—gently, reverently, just once.

A soft, impatient noise rose from the back of her throat, and she grabbed the collar of his shirt. "You said yes to warm hands and hot kisses," she whispered.

He grinned against her mouth. "I always keep my promises."

The second kiss melted them both. She opened for him with a soft sigh, and he took his time. Tasting her. Stroking his hands down her back. Letting her clutch his shoulders as if he were the only reason she didn't fall over.

And then—because he wanted this to be good, so damn good—he pulled back enough to look her in the eyes. "You set the pace."

Ginny blinked, breathless. "You're really putting me in charge?"

"I'll follow orders until you tell me otherwise."

She tilted her head thoughtfully. "In that case—less talking, more touching."

He chuckled and obeyed, sliding his hands under her shirt, savouring the warm skin he found. When he reached the edge of her bra, she arched into him.

"Do you have any idea how much I like your boobs?" he murmured then bent to kiss her collarbone. "They're perfect. Absolutely unfair."

"You're welcome," she said with a laugh.

He eased her shirt over her head, kissing every new inch of exposed skin. The flush in her chest, the swell of her breasts—God, he could spend a lifetime exploring. She wasn't posing. Wasn't pretending. She just *was*. Real and open and beautiful.

"Top ten best things I've ever seen," he whispered reverently as he nudged the bra up and kissed along the curve of her breast.

She laughed again, delighted and surprised. "Only top ten?"

"Well, I might need to test drive them for a while to be sure," he said and ran his tongue across her nipple until she gasped.

She shoved at his shoulder, mock outraged. "You're impossible."

He dropped them both onto the bunk, her laughing, him

grinning, and the two of them tangled together in an awkward, glorious heap.

"Hey!" she squeaked as he hooked his fingers behind her knees and ran his fingertips down her bare calves. "What are you doing?"

"Testing a theory." Because this was Ginny, and the thing between them was fire and heat yet still family in all the right ways. Which meant this too was as necessary as breathing.

"What theory?"

"That your feet are still ticklish."

"Don't you dare—Tucker Stewart!"

She shrieked as he tickled her arch with one wicked finger, holding her down to enjoy the sensation of her whole body squirming under him. Childish memories turning into adult delight as every brush together lit his desire hotter.

Laughter burst free. "Stop, stop—okay, okay, *mercy!*"

He stilled immediately, grinning at her, all flushed and breathless. "That was satisfying."

"You're evil."

"I'm motivated."

Her smile gentled, and she reached for him, threading her fingers through his hair. "Then show me."

Tucker stripped her slowly, worshipfully, one layer at a time. She helped him—unhurried, unashamed. Her hips rolled against his hands, her laughter quieter now, replaced with breathy little gasps and the occasional whisper in his ear that nearly undid him.

He undressed only enough to stay grounded—this wasn't about him right now, but God, her hands on his torso were wicked pleasure.

When she lay before him, bare and golden in the low light, he ran a hand down her side, fingers reverent.

"I want you to feel everything," he said softly. "And I want you to know—this *is* because I want you. Not as a distraction. Not as an escape."

Ginny looked up at him, her eyes dark and unguarded. "Then make me feel, Tucker."

So he did.

He kissed his way down her body, slow and thorough. He paused at her breasts, letting his tongue trace circles that made her arch. He buried his face against them, savouring every curve, every sound she made.

Then lower.

Ginny cried out softly as his mouth found her sex. Her thighs tensed, her fingers threaded through his hair, her back arched. He didn't stop. Not when she begged, not when she whispered his name.

"Goddess. You're so gorgeous." He used his fingertips to stroke with slow, teasing precision, then slipped two fingers inside her, the rhythm building in time with his tongue. The sounds she made echoed in the trailer until he was hard and aching and so turned on he was ready to explode without a single touch.

When she finally shattered, it was with a sob and a laugh, her body trembling under his hands.

Tucker rested his forehead against her belly, one arm wrapped around her waist. His head was spinning. Hopefully she was as off-kilter as he was.

"Stars?" he asked, the word coming out breathless.

"Whole galaxies," she whispered. She stroked her fingers through his hair gently once, twice, then tightened her grip so she could angle his head toward her. "Your turn."

6

─────

She hadn't expected to feel this light.

Not after this day, where grief had pressed into every breath, with too much whiskey-soaked sugar, the sharp sting of off-key singing, and the quiet desperation of keeping her best friend from staging a one-woman floor show. Not even after *that* kiss—careful, hot, and full of history—had she thought lightness was even possible.

But here she was. Naked. Warm. Tangled in Tucker's arms in the dim, hay-scented interior of the horse trailer. Laughter lingered in her throat, and her skin tingled with pleasure.

"You're warm," he murmured against her hair, arms locked tight around her as she shifted against him. "That blanket's doing overtime."

She smiled into his shoulder, body curled close. "Might be me. I've been told I run hot."

"Can confirm."

His voice was low, rumbling through her bones in the best way. She tilted her head, brushed her lips against his in a teasing kiss. "Then let's turn up the heat."

His eyes darkened, though the smile didn't leave his mouth. "Bossy."

"Motivated," she echoed, throwing his earlier words right back at him.

The next kiss found its way easily, slow and exploratory at first. Their mouths met in lazy rhythm, tongue stroking against tongue, hands wandering over skin like reacquainting with a favorite map. But the trailer was cramped, and as desire built, space became a problem.

Tucker eased himself onto the edge of the bunk, feet braced, legs spread to make room. Ginny straddled him, settling on his thighs, her knees bracketing his hips. It took some manoeuvering.

"Okay, wait—your leg there—no, not like that—ow, my elbow—" she half laughed-half grunted as her shoulder hit the tack wall and her knee smacked into the saddle bench.

Tucker grinned. "Sexy."

She drew back with mock offense. "Are you mocking my trailer seduction technique?"

"Never. Just admiring the display of coordination."

"Good. Burn it into your brain." Her eyes sparkled as she arched an eyebrow. "You'll want to remember this forever."

And then he kissed her again—hard, deep, the kind of kiss that made her forget she had knees, never mind where the trailer's walls were.

"Hang on," he murmured, reaching behind him to rummage through his duffel. His fingers closed around something, and he pulled it out with a victorious smile.

She squinted. "A condom?"

"Emergency stash."

Relief melted into gratitude. "Colour me impressed."

He turned the wrapper over then winced. "Shit."

Damn it. If something was wrong, she didn't have any backup condoms nearby. "What?"

"These were supposed to be a gag gift. For Luke's birthday. They're—uh—glow in the dark."

She blinked. Then amusement flooded in and she laughed, the sound breaking over them full of delight. "Oh my God. That's perfect."

"Seriously?"

"Well, mentioning my brother during sex is officially off-limits in the future, but yes. The condom is absolutely perfect. Use it."

He groaned but laughed too as he tore the wrapper open and slid it on. And then he was beneath her again, and nothing else mattered.

She shifted her hips, breath catching as he slid inside. The stretch of it, the heat—it was overwhelming and grounding all at once. Their foreheads pressed together, and everything stilled for a heartbeat.

"God, Tucker."

"Still good?" His voice was hoarse.

"Spectacular."

They found their rhythm quickly—slow to start, a rocking sync that matched the years they'd danced around this. But tension built fast, each movement steeped in years of repressed want, and soon his hands were clutching her hips, guiding her down onto him harder, deeper.

She rose to meet him, twisted her angle just slightly, and when he groaned against her skin, she laughed breathlessly, triumphant. Driving him to the edge was its own kind of pleasure.

His hand slipped between them.

Her breath hitched. "Oh—"

He found her clit with maddening precision, circling,

pressing, teasing until her thighs quivered and her breath became uneven.

"Tucker—"

"Let go," he whispered against her skin. "Come again for me, goddess."

She did. Her body bowed as release slammed through her, her cry muffled against his throat. He followed, hips thrusting up with desperate rhythm, his own release tearing from his chest in a low shout.

They stayed like that for a long, hazy moment—clinging, panting, sweat-slicked skin pressed close.

Ginny shifted and her shoulder bumped the light switch on the wall.

Click.

The overhead light snapped off. The faint glimmer filtering in from the yard light was just enough to reveal a soft, pulsing glow between their bodies. Ginny blinked, then leaned back to check.

Her laughter broke the silence. "Oh my God. It really *does* glow."

Tucker dropped his forehead onto her shoulder with a groan. "Never living this down."

"You mean *I'm* never going to survive. This is golden fodder for girl gossip, and I can't tell a soul."

He muttered something unintelligible, kissed her shoulder anyway, then reached for a towel from the bench. They cleaned up together, slow and gentle, trading quiet kisses and sleepy grins.

They curled back under the blanket, Ginny tucked against his chest. For the first time in a long, long while, she let herself truly rest.

She woke to soft fingers tracing down her spine and Tucker's lips brushing her temple.

"Hey," he whispered. "It's just past four. You should sneak back into the house before the ranch starts moving."

She blinked then stretched languidly, skin sliding over his, muscles humming. She'd go for a ride this morning. Pretend she was in the barn all night or something. "I *also* said I wanted to turn off my brain and just feel." She pushed up onto an elbow. "And I'm not quite done with that yet."

He grinned as she rolled back over him, this time more confident, more fluid. No elbow collisions or cramped limbs— just want, and warmth, and the easy rediscovery of shared pleasure.

It was quick, but full of feeling. Familiar, sweet, with little gasps of pleasure and whispered encouragement. Ginny came first, her face buried in his neck, and Tucker followed a breath later with a low moan and his fist clenched in the blanket.

They lay tangled, catching their breath. The trailer was still dim, winter dawn hours away from lighting the edges of the sky.

"We need a proper getaway," Ginny offered when she finally got off the bed and reached for her underwear. "An actual trip. Tent, cabin, motel—hell, even a yurt."

Tucker blinked at her, dragging on his shirt. "Yurt?"

"I'm saying I'm flexible. I can rough it. As long as there's a shower nearby, I'm in."

He sat up, dragging his fingers through his hair. "Chances are I'm going to be in Manitoba for the foreseeable future."

"Then we meet somewhere in the middle," she said easily. "Once a year for sure. Just us. No promises. Just...*this*."

His heart tightened, a strange mix of ache and awe. "And if one of us is with someone?"

"Then we don't," she said, voice steady. "No drama. No regrets. But if we're both free..."

"We're on," he finished.

They nodded and sealed the deal with a quiet understanding.

"And whenever you're at Silver Stone," she added as she tugged her boots on, "we're friends first. First and always, got it?"

He stood, took her hand, and pulled her in for one last kiss. "You're one in a million, goddess."

Her grin curled, slow and pleased. "I like that nickname."

"I like you."

She kissed him again, soft and certain. "I'm glad you're mine."

Not forever. Not in every sense. But for now. For this night, this morning, the foreseeable future.

A sliver of stolen time—it was more than enough to be a start.

IF YOU'D LIKE to find out how Ginny and Tucker's story concludes, check out **A Rancher's Love** in the Stones of Heart Falls series.

GIFTS OF THE HEART

After dating for over six months, Kevin is looking for more than casual fun and flirting with Edison. Only his colourful butterfly of a boyfriend is commitment phobic, and Kevin isn't about to hurt the most tender-hearted, sweetest, and sexiest man he's ever met by pushing boundaries.

Which puts holiday gift giving squarely in Edison's corner. Can Edison push past his fears and find a very Kevin *and* Edison approved way to admit he's ready for more?

Starring: Kevin Robb (psychiatrist at High Water) and Edison Whorlen (nurse at the Heart Falls Community Health Clinic).

Featuring: The High Water crew: Aiden & Petra Skye and their newly adopted teenage daughter Jinx. Tansy & Jake Skye and their son Jeffrey. Sydney Jeremiah and Declan Skye. Plus Fern Gabrielle and random people around town and the crew at the firehall Christmas party.

Basically, a lot of Heart Falls came out for this one!

Timeline: This scene is set in December after the end of **A Cowboy's Claim**.

1

───────

Early December, High Water ranch

The weight of the day slid off his shoulders as Kevin Robb settled to one side of the double-wide Adirondack chair. He stretched his legs toward the fire pit as dusky smoke twisted on the air. It was oddly satisfying to have successfully lit the fire and have flames licking over the wood like bright, dancing sprites.

Coming to work at High Water ranch nearly a year ago had been just what the doctor ordered. It had given Kevin time to recover from the unexpected attack he'd survived from an unruly patient. Given him time to get his own head on straight and be ready for when life gave him something better than lemons.

Over the next half hour, the rest of the ranch strolled up in ones and twos and found spots to relax.

Aiden and Petra arrived with Jinx in tow. Or maybe it was the other way around as the seventeen-year-old imperiously pointed to chairs on the right side of the fire, and her newly official parents happily sat as ordered.

"Hey, Kev." Jinx curled up in the chair to his left, Dixie the golden retriever at her feet as always. "Nice fire."

"Thanks. Better than the last time I was in charge when it spent more time smoldering than burning."

She nodded, wiggling her fingers in greeting at the two ranch hands—aka, the current guests taking advantage of High Water's secret halfway house.

The men dipped their heads politely then sat on the opposite side of the fire.

Were they staying away from Jinx? Or staying away from him?

Kevin wasn't sure. Not everyone felt comfortable around him, thinking maybe his psychiatric training meant he could read their minds.

Nope, although there were times he wished he could.

Another of their core group arrived. Sydney settled into her chair with a happy sigh. "Declan and Logan are on their way as soon as they finish the dishes. Tansy and Jake are staying at her sister's after supper, so they and Jeffrey won't be here tonight."

"Is Edison joining us?" Jinx asked Kevin.

"Hope so," Kevin told her.

He and Edison had been dating since last February, more frequently since the summer. Only in the last month or two had Edison finally accepted the invitation to join the High Water family for dinner or the evening afterward.

Petra and Jinx pulled out crochet projects as Aiden tuned his guitar. When Declan and Logan arrived a few minutes later, Edison walked beside them.

A zing of happiness rushed over Kevin, and he snorted softly. It never ceased to astonish him how the mere sight of Edison got to him.

Kevin rose to his feet to greet the man.

Edison's lips curled with mischief. "Such a gentleman."

The kiss Edison pressed to his cheek—brief yet warm—made Kevin want to show some decidedly un-gentlemanly behavior with a far more demonstrative kiss.

For now, though, Kevin held back and simply gestured to the open space beside him on the love seat. "Saved you a spot," he told Edison quietly. "Glad you could make it."

"Glad to be here." Edison's thigh pressed firmly against Kevin's even as he turned to speak to Sydney. "The adult first-aid class I taught today went well."

"I spotted no smoke on the horizon, so you didn't burn down any buildings. Score is in your favour," Sydney teased.

"I know, right?" Edison dramatically pressed a hand to his chest. "Go me."

"We can't all be as destructive as the best," Sydney offered with a rueful laugh.

Declan shook his head as he poked the fire with a stick. "Where did you teach the class since we don't have a community hall anymore?"

"The school gave me a classroom," Edison said. "It was crowded and we had to move the desks twice, but it mostly worked. It's going to be tough doing without the hall. I never realized how many activities took place there over the year."

Quiet conversations drifted between people as the low notes of guitar switched from single notes to melody, and Aiden hummed softly as he played. Guitar music wove around them like a warm blanket that enclosed the group with a cozy, protective feeling. Gentle conversations and sharing made for a relaxing evening.

Around ten, the group slowly headed off in different directions.

Aiden crooked a finger at Petra. "Come on, baby mama. You need to catch up on some sleep."

Petra accepted the hand he held to her even as she glanced Kevin's way and offered a knowing wink. She was sharp enough to figure out Kevin was hoping for a little privacy with Edison.

Both the ranch hands left after offering quiet goodnights. Logan yawned as he waved lazily. "I'm done, too. Night all."

Declan and Sydney followed a few minutes later.

Sydney offered a teasing glance over her shoulder. "Don't stay too long, Edison, or you'll be late to open the clinic tomorrow."

"As if." Edison tilted his head. "I'm the punctual prince of medicine, and you know it."

"You're a caffeine-fueled menace," Sydney tossed back. "But I couldn't do it without you. Good night."

Only Jinx and Dixie remained. She stretched then swung the reusable shopping bag that held her yarn and crochet project over her shoulder. "I'm calling it a night as well. I'm off to Sasha's tomorrow to work on a group project on renewable energy."

"You're going to nail that," Edison told her. "*You're* the ultimate renewable energy source."

Jinx laughed as her golden retriever nudged Edison for a pat and got a full-body cuddle in return. Edison murmured something low to the dog before he straightened and accepted the hug Jinx offered.

"You're a sweetheart, Edison."

"Takes one to know one," he offered back, light-hearted joy in his tone.

Kevin didn't move. Didn't speak. But when Jinx turned and gave him a nod—brief, quiet, but absolutely deliberate—something loosened in his chest.

Edison resettled a moment later, legs folding underneath himself with that relaxed grace Kevin had come to love. Without a word, Edison slipped his hand into Kevin's, and they both stared into the fire.

Thoughts raced through Kevin's head like a train at top speed.

"You know that hug means a lot, yeah?" Kevin finally said softly.

Edison twisted to face Kevin, his wide brown eyes shadowed by the firelight. "Yeah. I think so."

"Jinx doesn't do that. Not with men outside her family. Not easily."

"She's healing. You can see it in the way she stands straighter now. Trust comes slowly, but...when it comes, it's real." Edison's voice was quiet, no louder than the wind pushing against their backs. He stared into Kevin's eyes. "You guys did that. Made a place for her to become strong. It's been a privilege to watch her bloom, even from the sidelines."

Kevin looked at him—at his tousled curls and soft sweatshirt, eyeliner smudged slightly at the corners after the long day. Gorgeous, but also so much more than the visible flamboyant outer shell. Edison's warmth was like a candle burning through frosted glass. People noticed it. Trusted it.

"I can see why she picked you," Kevin said.

Edison leaned closer until his shoulder bumped Kevin's. "You're a cutie, you know."

A slow smile curved Kevin's lips. "I know."

They sat in silence for a while, just watching the fire.

Kevin didn't mind silence. He often lived in it, professionally and personally, but with Edison it never felt empty. It was just a different kind of conversation.

Eventually, Edison stirred. "There's a new exhibit opening

at Gabrielle's art gallery soon. The flyer said it's called *Winter's Wonderland* or something poetic like that."

Kevin hummed. "Holiday-themed?"

"I guess? I'm picturing cozy snow scenes and glittery icicles. Knowing how Chance tries to make the shows community friendly, I bet there'll be at least one painting of a grumpy Santa stuck in a chimney." Edison squeezed his hand. "We should go."

"I'd like that."

More silence. Then—

"Hypothetically," Edison said, far too casually, "what's the best Christmas gift you've ever gotten?"

Kevin didn't answer right away. Instead, he let himself lean back more fully into the chair, Edison curled against his side, hand warm and steady in Kevin's.

Childhood Christmases had been solid but not lavish. A new bike. A winter coat. A game that he'd really wanted. In his adult years he'd discovered he was drawn to a more minimalistic lifestyle and leaned toward spending money on events and adventures rather than things.

For a while, the consumer-driven focus of the holiday had annoyed him—it had taken deliberate work to let that judgment go and allow others to celebrate how they pleased and find his own joy in the season again.

He didn't want to say any of that. If the little knickknacks and sweets and other things he'd offered Kevin over the past months were any hint—

Edison's love language was gifts.

"I think the best one I ever got was a copy of *Into the Wild,*" Kevin said finally. This wasn't the time to explain why such a book about such a terrible, tragic idea was so important. "From my dad. I still have it on the shelf."

Edison made a pleased little noise. "Books are good. Thoughtful. Personal."

"Thinking of giving me a book?"

"I wasn't thinking of giving you anything." Edison offered the cheerful lie. "Although I would love it if you had another scarf to look sexy in."

Kevin chuckled. "You think I'm sexy in scarves?"

Edison tilted his head and batted his lashes. "Kevin, I think you're sexy wearing a disapproving scowl. Add a scarf? You're lethal."

It couldn't be resisted. Kevin curled his hand around the back of Edison's neck and drew him forward for a kiss.

Warm lips pressed to his, Edison eagerly took the offering, opening his mouth with a sigh.

Kevin kept it in control and deliberately light because tonight wasn't the time to be getting hot and heavy. But this kiss? This moment? It was as necessary as breathing as Edison's sweet taste rushed in and sent a thousand dreams flying.

Kevin didn't want a book. Not this year. What he wanted was this—Edison's laughter and light and the way he looked at Kevin as if there was a future waiting for them.

Kevin's gut clenched. But as much as he wanted that future, it wasn't what *Edison* had signed up for.

Since day one, Edison had made it clear he wasn't looking for permanence. His past was full of complications, he'd said, so he chose to live in the present—joyfully, deliberately, beautifully.

Kevin understood that. Hell, his job meant he was trained to respect that with every inch of his soul.

But tonight, with Edison beside him and the holiday season closing in on them, Kevin wanted more than good intentions and warm blankets. He wanted to give *Edison* something that mattered.

Something that didn't say *I love you* and throw the other man into a panic, but said *I see you. I get you. I'm here.*

I'd like to always be here.

Kevin wasn't sure what that gift looked like yet, but he'd figure it out. Soon, because Edison was the best thing that had happened to him in a long, long time.

And Kevin? He was more than willing to fight, quietly and carefully, for someone worth holding on to.

2

____

*E*dison walked into the Heart Falls Medical Clinic, flipped the lights on, and gave the coffee pot a suspicious glare.

The contraption was set on a timer by the front-desk staff, supposedly to be ready when the clinic opened. Jenny tended to set the clock for far too early, so the finished coffee sat on the hot plate getting evil and nasty.

Secretly, Edison was grateful that the power occasionally went out on the Main Street block and messed with the electronics.

"Insult to caffeine," he muttered. He sniffed at the full pot, considered the affront to his taste buds, then made an executive decision.

He happily set about remaking the batch. The admin staff wouldn't arrive for another twenty minutes, and the doctor on call—Lexie today—habitually arrived one minute before the doors opened.

Once the new coffee was brewing, he did a walk-through. Unlocked the medical safe. Checked each of the two examination rooms to make sure they were stocked, tidy, and ready for the day. Edison liked having the building to himself for a little while, and the opening actions he followed were routine and familiar, the scent of antiseptic the perfect perfume.

He'd opened the clinic many times before, but this morning felt different. As if something quietly electric hummed under his skin. Maybe it was the way Kevin's hand had lingered in his even as the fire burned low last night. Maybe it was the kisses they'd shared—sweet, deliberate, yet charged like a promise he didn't quite know how to read.

Maybe it was the way Kevin had *looked* at him.

Lordy, his brain was going to explode if he didn't find a way to settle his racing thoughts.

When Lexie breezed in with her usual energetic *hello*, Edison poured her a cup of non-offensive coffee and forced himself into his groove.

Appointments were steady. Minor complaints and follow-ups, a flu shot or three, and one toddler who proudly told Edison he was going to be a race car when he grew up. Not drive one—*be* one.

Edison saluted him and said that he too hoped to be that fast one day.

By ten-thirty, he was in the break room on his scheduled pause, checking out the tabs he'd left open the night before with Christmas gift ideas. None of them felt quite right. The leather wallet he'd found was gorgeous, but Kevin had a serviceable wallet, worn, yet still in good shape. The ceramic mugs made Edison smile, and he could picture Kevin using them, but the man seemed happy with the set he already owned.

A *ping* interrupted his thoughts. Incoming video call. He glanced at the screen.

Mom & Dad.

He connected then propped his phone on a small box of exam gloves, adjusting the camera so his face was front and center. Lordy, his curls were far too dramatic today.

"Hi, baby!" His mom's face appeared, cheerful as always, framed by a fuzzy sweater collar and her trademark hoop earrings. "You look cozy."

"I'm at work," Edison said, laughing.

"And yet, cozy," his dad called from the background. "That scrub jacket is doing overtime. Are those rabbits and rainbows? Sweet."

Edison glanced down then back up at his father in astonishment. "How is it possible that you spotted those details in under two seconds?"

"I can feel it through the screen. It's got soul."

Edison rolled his eyes affectionately. "You're a menace. Where are you guys—at home or babysitting my niblings?"

"At home for now. Snowed a bit this morning. I had to knock three inches off the bird feeder," Mom said. "How's Heart Falls?"

"Cold, but no new snow. Busy. Good."

Dad leaned in for a second. "I'm heading to the hardware store but have to dig us out before I can use the driveway. I'll leave you two to gossip, but before I go—" He pointed straight at Edison. "That photo you sent. You and the guy at the waterfall?"

"Kevin," Edison said.

"You look good together," his dad said straight up. "Real good. Thinkin' of bringing him home for Christmas?"

Edison blinked. "That's a big question."

His dad grinned. "It's only a four-hour drive. Liam and Tisha will be over with the kids. With six adults and two munchkins, we can have a proper snowball fight."

His mom elbowed him. "Go on, work your shovel. I want real gossip."

"Love you, sweet pea!" Dad said before his grin slowly widened to epic proportions. "Know what snowmen eat for breakfast? Frosted Flakes."

Edison groaned. "Love you, Pop, but you're terrible."

His mom waited until the door closed behind her then leaned in and inspected Edison more closely. "Now. Did you want to talk about Kevin?"

Edison flopped back into his chair with a sigh, his face heating even though it was just his mom on the other side of the screen. "Kev and I are...good."

"That sounded like a question."

"No." He made a face. "Yes. *Ugh*."

His mom didn't push. She just waited, the corners of her lips curling into a half smile.

"He's wonderful," Edison said finally. "Steady. Thoughtful. Sexy as hell in a sweater. And he listens. Not in the way that makes me feel as if I'm being analyzed—even though that's exactly what he does for a living—but in the way that makes me want to say more."

"And this scares you?"

Edison nodded. "Yeah. Kinda does."

"Because?"

"Because I let myself be hurt." The words came out before he could catch them, and the echo of his high school sweetheart's name whispered through his brain. He'd tried his best to avoid thinking about Lenny since the fallout. "I know it was almost fifteen years ago, but I still feel the pain at times. I swore I wouldn't let it happen again. That was part of the deal I made with myself. No one gets to be as close as Lenny. No one gets to rewrite my script for me."

"And yet," Mom said gently.

"And yet." Edison looked away. "Kevin is kind. The real kind. The hard kind. Like, he doesn't talk much, but he remembers everything. He's not trying to fix me, or reshape me, or dim me down. He just sees me. I don't know what to do with that."

Her smile softened. "So you let it happen slowly. The same way you've done everything else. When you wanted to go to nursing school, you didn't just jump. You asked questions. You tested the waters. You told your truth a little at a time, and you found out who could be trusted."

"Yeah, well. I also dyed my hair fire-engine red and wore glitter eyeliner to my first lab practical."

"I meant slowly *for you*."

Edison laughed, his heart easing a little.

She leaned forward, propping her chin in her palm. "Sounds as if you're already doing what needs to be done. You're spending time together and you're doing fun things." She paused, gaze drifting to one corner of the screen. "I won't ask about your sex life other than to remind you to be careful."

Edison's cheeks went hot, but she'd always been blunt and upfront, and he appreciated it as much now as when he was a confused teen. "Insert obligatory, *Yes, Mom*."

"If it's time for you to adjust your mandates, you'll know, baby. Your heart's too big to be tricked again. You just have to trust it."

"And if I get hurt?"

"Then you'll cry on the phone to your mom, and your father and I will come down and we'll eat our way through a tub of peppermint fudge swirl together. But if you *don't* get hurt—if this is the real thing, Edison—then it'll be worth every scary second."

The call ended with a flurry of *I love you*s and virtual hugs.

Edison sat alone in the quiet break room, hands around

what was now a lukewarm cup of coffee, and let himself breathe.

Then he pulled out his phone, typed a quick text, and hit Send before he could overthink it.

Edison: Wanted to make it an official request. You good to hit the art gallery with me on Friday? I'll make us dinner after.

His screen lit up with a reply less than a minute later.

Kevin: Love to.

Two words. That's all it was—but somehow Edison read much, much more into the message. It turned his insides warm and a little jittery.

Yet, as his mom had said, maybe that was a good thing.

3

———

The kitchen at High Water smelled like flour, cinnamon, and fresh snow. The combination didn't make sense, but Kevin had learned by now that a lot of things about this place worked exactly like that.

Unexpected. Unapologetic. Good for you, whether you realized it or not.

"Spheres," five-year-old Jeffrey intoned seriously, rolling a wad of dough on the tabletop. "The buns need to be round like spheres. Or eyeballs."

Kevin blinked. "Eyeballs?"

Jeffrey grinned, all gap-toothed and proud. "Mommy taught me 'bout spheres."

"Did she?" Kevin side-eyed her, amused.

Tansy smirked as she wiped her hands on a towel. "I also told him the key to fluffy dinner buns is to let them rise —*without* poking them too often. That lesson doesn't seem to be sinking in as hard."

"I *heard* her," Jeffrey whispered to Kevin as if it were a secret. "But my fingers want to poke anyway."

"Every scientist has that problem," Kevin said solemnly, earning a giggle.

Truth was, Kevin liked spending time with the kid. Baking was low-stakes chaos—yeast and flour and sugar turning into something warm and good. He liked having those things in his life.

Tansy hummed happily as she expertly prepped a second and third tray while they butchered their batch. "You home for dinner tonight?" she asked Kevin.

"Not tonight," Kevin said. "I've got plans."

"Oh?"

He nodded. "Art gallery winter exhibit."

Tansy raised an eyebrow. "Taking Edison?"

"He's taking me. Then dinner after at his place."

"What're you bringing?" She folded the dough in her hand and twisted, and it magically turned into a perfect ball. Sphere. Whatever.

Kevin opened his mouth. Closed it. "A bottle of wine," he offered after a beat.

"That's nice," Tansy said, but her tone held a mild challenge. He felt the nudge before she even added, "And?"

And nothing. That was the problem.

Kevin swallowed and leaned his hands on the edge of the island. He was the shit at finding gift ideas that were more than useless, meaningless trinkets. "I've been thinking about Christmas. About big picture stuff. I didn't even think to plan tonight properly."

Tansy turned, hands on her hips, head tilting. "You think he expects a grand gesture?"

"No. That's the thing. Edison doesn't make demands like that." Kevin stared at the flour-dusted counter. "But I want to give more. He deserves something that feels intentional."

"I like Edison." Jeffrey poked a bun squarely in the middle, all attention on his finger as it sank into the soft dough. "Is he your boyfriend?"

Tansy gasped dramatically. "Nosy question, little tyke."

Kevin couldn't help laughing. "It's okay. Yes. Edison's important to me."

"Good. I like him, too." Jeffrey nodded, completely satisfied. "I know he likes snacks. Oh! You should get him a snow globe. That would make him happy."

Kevin pressed his lips together. "We'll see."

Tansy leaned a hip against the counter. "You know, the gallery sells small prints and gift cards and hand-painted mugs. If you're dead set on picking something up."

He groaned. "I'm not great with 'things.' Not when it counts."

"Well, then forget the things," Tansy said, sharp and kind at the same time. "You're good at being present. At showing up. Do that."

Kevin let that sink in. *Do that.*

"I just..." He trailed off. "I don't want to screw this up."

"You won't," she said simply. "Not if you keep doing what you already do. Notice what he cares about. Listen. Ask him to show you what matters."

One of the ranch hands wandered into the house at that point, and the day slipped away with other tasks. Both the poked and unpoked buns were cooling on baking racks by the time Kevin left the house for the final time later that afternoon.

He stepped into the cool November sunshine, checked the bottle of wine in the car, then double-checked it. It didn't feel like enough, but at least it was something.

As he turned the ignition, he reminded himself. Eyes open. Ears open. Heart open.

Edison wouldn't demand anything. But Kevin was ready to offer it anyway.

Kevin pulled up to the small house Edison rented near the coulee on the far side of town. His overeager date was already waiting on the porch. The porch light glowed behind him as he bounced down the steps. A knit beanie was pulled low over his curls and a long red coat was zipped and belted tightly at his waist.

Kevin rolled down the window. "I was going to walk all the way to the door. You robbed me of a very romantic knock."

Edison grinned as he rushed forward. "I didn't want you peeking inside. I have surprises planned."

"That so?"

Edison opened the passenger door. "That is *so.*"

The scent of cinnamon and chocolate and good clean soap hovered around his passenger as Edison buckled in with deliberate care.

"You good?" Kevin asked.

Edison nodded. "Better than. You?"

Kevin chuckled. "Ask me again in two hours."

His date hummed softly, face going serious. "If the art show's not your thing, we could—"

"Not worried about the art," Kevin reassured him quickly. He reached across the space between them and squeezed Edison's fingers softly. "Don't mind me. My brain is tangling in knots for no reason. The company is fantastic, so the art could be crayon drawings for all I care."

He found a parking space on Main Street. The shops along the wooden boardwalk were lit up with strings of twinkle lights. The town looked festive and bright and happy, and as Edison slipped his hand around the crook of Kevin's elbow, some of the unwelcome nerves slid away.

Inside, the gallery was already half full. Coats rustled and boots squeaked and soft murmurs of appreciation floated beneath ambient music.

The first floor had been transformed into a winding series of angled walls and narrow hallways, each one holding small wonders. The wintery theme turned out to include a mix of old- and new-style paintings. Soft watercolours and dramatic oils, silent forests and snow-slick city streets. Some local, some classic.

Kevin moved slowly. Edison didn't.

Edison bounced from painting to painting with light on his face and commentary that blended art terms with delight. "Look at the light in this one—it's got that golden haze that screams contentment, don't you think?" Or, "I swear this exact birch grove lived in my childhood dreams." Then, "This guy? Painted snow the way it *feels*, not just how it looks. It's sticky and hushed and alive."

Kevin followed, not saying much. Just watching.

He didn't have Edison's vocabulary for brushstroke or palette, but he knew this—Edison *glowed* when he was excited, and not just metaphorically. His eyes got brighter. His posture taller. His laugh when something surprised him was like striking a match in a dark room.

At one small canvas depicting a train winding through mountain passes under northern lights, Edison stopped, fingers pressed dramatically to his chest. "This reminds me of a trip we took when I was twelve. I got to sit in the dome car. Everyone else was bored, but I watched snow hit the glass and thought it was magic."

Kevin couldn't stop himself. "You're kind of magic."

Edison turned to him with mock suspicion. "Was that flirting?"

"Maybe."

"You're out of practice."

"Am I?"

"Definitely."

Kevin leaned in just a little, his voice low. "That's okay. I have a good teacher. I promise I'll get better."

Edison beamed at him, all dimples and glitter-soft eyeshadow.

They made their way upstairs. Fern Gabrielle stood beside a VR setup and waved them over. Her prosthesis was decorated with bright red ribbon and a shiny red bow. "Afternoon, gentlemen. You ready to walk through some magical winter dreams?"

Edison stepped forward like a kid at an amusement park. "Every day of my life."

She slid headsets into their hands and adjusted the settings. "This program lets you move through actual landscapes used as references by the Group of Seven, and then their painting interpretations. It's a soft-footprint kind of time travel."

They took their places.

With the flick of a switch, Kevin was in a world of soft hush and swirling frost, beside Edison's avatar—a flickering outline with Edison's gestures and stance. In silence, they wandered across snowy fields, through pine forests rimmed with mist, over lakes frozen into glass.

At one point, Edison reached out—just a hand lift in real life—and in the VR world, it mirrored him perfectly.

"Would you look at that," Edison whispered, quiet with awe. "We're walking through brushstrokes."

Kevin didn't say much. He didn't need to. Edison's joy did the speaking for them both.

Later, out in the crisp night, Edison clutched Kevin's arm. "That was better than expected."

"Agreed."

"I mean—art and VR and snowy romance?" Edison bumped his shoulder gently. "If you'd brought me a snow globe, I might've swooned."

Kevin chuckled. Seems the kid this morning had been right. "Missed opportunity."

Edison looked up at him. "But you were here. That's what matters."

He couldn't stop himself. Kevin leaned in and kissed the man. Soft and tender and full of heart. Edison hummed happily, and when they pulled apart, Edison's eyes shone like stars.

The whole drive to Edison's, Kevin swore twinkling galaxies swirled inside the vehicle.

The house, small and neat, had lights glowing in the windows and mismatched furniture visible through sheer curtains. Inside, it smelled like cumin and garlic and roasted vegetables.

The kitchen was half open to the living space, with Edison's flair tucked into every corner. A string of paper snowflakes ran across the top of the window. Candles in odd glass jars. Art prints of constellations. A stack of board games on the table next to a record player spinning low jazz.

Kevin stood awkwardly, more aware than ever that he hadn't brought anything to make the night special. The wine, sure, but beyond that, he had no game plan. Just himself.

And yet—

Edison glanced from his spot in front of the stove with a warm look. Slowly, one brow drifted upward. "You're wearing your thinking face. Brain still running on overdrive?"

Kevin blinked. "Sorry. I'm...I don't know. Hoping I didn't screw up."

Edison paused, the spoon hanging precariously over the steaming pot. "Why would you think that?"

"Because I didn't bring anything but wine. Because I didn't plan something impressive." *Because I want this to matter and I'm not sure how to show that right now.*

After carelessly tossing the spoon onto a bright red plate, Edison walked to him slowly, carefully, and placed his palms flat against Kevin's chest. "You're here. You're honest. You let me drag you through snowy pine trees in a VR simulator and you listened to my commentary. You were wonderful."

Kevin looked at him—really looked. "You think so?"

Edison nodded. "Yeah. I do. And I'm glad you're here tonight."

That, more than any snow globe or present, was the moment that lodged deep in Kevin's chest and stayed.

Edison clapped his hands and tilted his head jauntily. "And now? Supper is nearly ready. Time to work."

Kevin took a slow, deep breath. He couldn't be sure of the future. He still hadn't cracked the code on what to give Edison for Christmas.

But he knew this much; tonight felt different. The air between them shifted—just slightly—but enough for Kevin to believe that something was unfolding.

Something important.

4

___

*E*dison couldn't stop smiling.

He'd been smiling since the moment Kevin showed up with that serious expression that made Edison's chest ache in the best way. Since the moment Kevin's fingers brushed his as they stepped into the gallery, warm and sure. Since Kevin had kissed him after the exhibit. No words, but a dictionary's worth of meaning in his touch.

By the time they'd stepped through the front door of his home, Edison's cheeks hurt from how much he'd been grinning.

And now? With Kevin rolling up his sleeves like the literal fantasy he was? Edison might need to lie down.

Distraction was needed, now. "Plates are there. Glasses in the top cabinet. Forks in the drawer to your right," Edison reminded him before switching into danger mode. "And I swear, if you rearrange anything, I will haunt you."

"Yes, Chef." Kevin obligingly opened the correct doors and got to work. "I haven't changed anything the other times I've been here," he teased.

That was true. Which had to mean ironclad willpower on

his part, since Kevin's rooms at High Water were so spic-and-span tidy. Edison was always tempted to mess something up.

Hmmm. Which said more about Edison's issues than Kevin's.

Still, Edison gave him an approving nod. "Part of the reason you keep getting invited back," he shared with more honesty than intended.

The kitchen was small, but everything in it was his. A deep red tea towel hung off the oven handle, and the small round table bore a hand-stitched runner he'd found at a thrift shop in Edmonton. The mismatched plates were vintage, and his wine glasses were etched with tiny maple leaves.

Everything in the room made him happy inside. As Kevin moved around the space like he belonged there—quiet, calm, competent—he too made the *makes Edison happy* list.

The man had loosened his collar, and those sleeves—

Lord help me. Those sleeves were now rolled up just high enough to show off strong forearms and the faintest peek of veins.

Edison fanned himself dramatically as he brought over the sautéed vegetables. "You're dangerous like this. Casual domesticity looks illegally hot on you."

Kevin glanced up, expression amused. "I'm pretty sure I just set out cutlery."

"With *authority*," Edison said. "It's the authority that kills me."

They sat across from each other at the little table, knees brushing every time either of them shifted. The meal was simple but warm—creamy polenta with garlicky mushrooms, cumin-roasted squash, and a caramelized onion jam Edison had made last weekend because apparently he was a man who made jam now.

One bite in and Kevin moaned in approval. "You're spoiling me."

"I told you when we started dating; I come with snacks," Edison offered primly. "Also—flair, sparkle, and occasional bursts of musical theatre."

"I like all of that."

Edison's heart did that fluttery thing again, and he tried not to let it show too obviously.

Conversation was easy. Kevin listened like always—focused and present—but he also responded more tonight. Teased a little. Shared more stories. A brightness shone in his eyes Edison hadn't seen before, and it made anything feel possible.

When they'd finished their plates and Kevin started gathering the dishes, Edison caught his wrist.

"Sit. Please." He smiled. "I'll deal with the dishes tomorrow. Tonight feels too nice to waste on ordinary chores."

Kevin sat agreeably, that unreadable expression settling across his face.

"You okay?" Edison asked softly.

"Yeah." Kevin nodded slowly before rotating his palm up and letting their fingers mesh together. "I was just thinking how good this feels."

"Yeah," Edison echoed. "Me too."

"I like your place." Kevin glanced around but his gaze returned quickly to Edison's eyes. "I like being here with you."

A pause. Just long enough to make Edison's squirrel-chasing brain leap five trees and change direction completely.

Boom, they were freefalling into dangerous territory. "You don't feel like it's too much?"

Do you think that I'm too much?

Those words didn't come out of his mouth. He swore they didn't, but Kevin stared at him as if he'd spoken them clearly.

A soft squeeze to his fingers was followed by Kevin's firm

but gentle answer. "You are an amazing man. You're kind and fun and centered in yourself. When I look around your place, I see a reflection of that."

A knot formed in Edison's throat. "Someone told me I should stop flitting around and grow up." He paused. "They also told me that, in spite of being eighteen and having figured this part out, they didn't think we should be gay anymore. So I know they were wrong about—"

Kevin swore. "They told you to stop being gay? That's bullshit. Who had the balls to try that nonsense? Because I know it wasn't your parents. They're rock solid and a hoot."

"My high school boyfriend," Edison admitted quietly.

Across from him, Kevin's eyes widened then his whole body sagged slightly. "Definitely bullshit, but damn. I bet that hurt."

Edison eyed him for a second. "Don't pull your Dr. Robb analysis hat on me or anything, okay?"

"I won't," Kevin promised even as he leaned forward. "But I am sorry you had to deal with that crap as a teenager. Those years are hard enough without people we care about making it even more confusing."

"Amen," Edison agreed.

"Also, I'm very glad you're gay," Kevin announced with complete deadpan.

A snicker escaped before Edison could stop it.

Kevin tilted his head. "Not to change the topic or anything, but you were stretching your neck earlier. At the gallery. I meant to ask."

Edison waved his free hand. "Ugh. I helped Mr. and Mrs. Braxton move some stuff during my lunch break. It turned out to be mostly sandbags. Apparently, they're prepping for basement leaks again."

Kevin blinked. "Sandbags?"

"Yup. Heavy and awkward. It wasn't what I expected to help with, but..." Edison shrugged. "They're old enough the task might have hurt them. I wasn't going to let them throw their backs out when all it cost me was some sore muscles."

Kevin stood again, using the connection between them to tug Edison upward. "Come on."

Edison let himself be guided to his feet. "Where are we going?"

"Bedroom," Kevin said, his voice soft but firm. "You're getting a backrub."

A pleased noise escaped before Edison could bury it. "You know how to sweet-talk a man."

His room was just off the kitchen. The walls were painted soft cream, and the bed was covered with a thick quilt he'd sewn himself—fabrics collected over the years, memories stitched together in navy, burnt orange, and forest green.

Kevin guided him to sit on the edge of the bed then slowly unbuttoned his shirt. Edison shivered—not just from the cool air on his skin but from the reverent way Kevin's fingers moved, brushing his shoulders as he slid the fabric down and off.

"You always smell good," Kevin murmured, thumbs pressing gently along the muscles of Edison's upper back. "Like cedar and something warm."

"Fancy shampoo and a lifetime of good decisions," Edison said, but his voice was already going breathy.

Kevin hummed in amusement and leaned down, brushing his lips to the nape of Edison's neck.

Lordy, it felt amazing, and they'd only just begun.

A minute later Kevin had him positioned on his belly on the bed, crawling over him to place one knee on either side of Edison's thighs.

The massage started slowly. Gentle circles at first, then deeper pressure. Kevin's hands were strong and sure. He found every knot, every tight line of muscle, and coaxed it into ease. Edison melted, a soft moan escaping as Kevin's thumbs dug in just beneath his shoulder blades.

"You did too much today," Kevin scolded.

"I like helping people."

"I know. But maybe let someone take care of you, too."

The words hit like an arrow straight to the heart. Edison's breath caught.

Then Kevin's mouth followed his hands, kisses replacing pressure, lips ghosting over bare skin. A slow burn lit up along Edison's spine.

He turned slightly, enough to look up at Kevin.

"Are you trying to seduce me, Mr. Robb?"

Kevin smiled, slow and devastating. "Would it be working?"

Edison surged up to kiss him, hand curling into Kevin's shirt. Their lips met, slow and hungry. Kevin guided him gently back, kissing him again as they lined up together on the bed. Helpless to stop, Edison pulsed his hips forward, need swelling as the kiss deepened. As Kevin slid a hand to Edison's lower back and lined up their groins so perfectly—cock to cock, pressure rising.

"Kev. Don't stop," Edison begged.

Their hips moved in rhythm as heat built between them.

Kevin pulled back, and Edison cursed softly.

The other man smiled, but his expression also held want. A need as deep as Edison's. Kevin whispered, "Let me take care of you tonight."

Edison nodded, his throat too thick with emotion to answer properly. He trusted Kevin. He wanted this.

Wanted *him*.

What followed was delightful torment. Kevin's pace was patient but determined, a feather-light touch one moment and more grounding the next. He eased Edison's pants and underwear off, eyes dark and full of—

Something Edison refused to name. The mere idea still made his chest ache with how much he wanted to believe this was more.

One kiss after another, Kevin worked his way down Edison's body. Fingers ghosted over skin gone sensitive and hot. Little nips and hot strokes of Kevin's tongue were mixed with addictive pleasure as a strong fist wrapped around Edison's cock.

"*Kev...*"

A request? A promise? Edison didn't know what he was asking for, but when Kevin's mouth slipped over his shaft—hot, soft, and unhurried—Edison arched, fingers fisting the quilt, breath coming in ragged little gasps.

It was exquisite. Not only the physical sensations, but the intimacy. The *knowing*. Kevin kissed and licked and teased as if he wanted Edison to feel *worshipped*. As if every moment was a conversation they were having with skin and breath instead of words.

When Edison finally came, it was with a shudder that racked his entire body and a cry that he tried to muffle but didn't quite manage to hide.

Kevin held him as he came down. Just held him. Hands warm on Edison's back, breath soft against his hair. No demands. No pressure. Just presence. They lay tangled together in the aftermath, skin cooling, breath slowing.

"Wow," Edison whispered.

"Yeah," Kevin said, voice low and rough. "You're incredible."

Edison chuckled weakly. "That was... You're very good at massages, Dr. Robb."

Kevin chuckled as he pressed a kiss to his temple. "Don't

tell anyone at the clinic. They'll start booking me out." They lay in silence for a while longer before Kevin whispered, almost too quiet to hear, "I really like being here with you."

Edison's heart did that dangerous flutter again. He didn't know where this was going. He had rules and mandates, but maybe...

In this moment, in this room, with Kevin beside him and a quiet stillness wrapping around them like a second quilt—

It was enough to start dreaming about moving forward with new rules.

And maybe, just maybe, that was all he needed to know for now.`

5

———————

The message from Edison came in late Wednesday evening as Kevin was organizing work files on his laptop.

> Edison: Hope your day was as gorgeous as you! I'm making the rounds tomorrow after work to drop off some holiday goodies—if I don't get it done now, it'll all pile up. Just a heads-up in case you try to get a hold of me because my hands will either be full or I'll be out of service range.

Kevin stared at the screen for a beat, smiled, then typed back:

> Kevin: Want some company? I'm free.

There was a pause—three dots, then none. Then back again.

Edison: You sure? I'd love that. But I've got, like, more than a dozen stops and a car that already smells like Willy Wonka's Candy factory vomited in the back seat.

Kevin: Perfect. I'll bring hot chocolate.

Edison: You're on.

Thursday evening, Kevin slipped into the passenger seat of Edison's compact SUV and handed over a peppermint hot chocolate. The scent of baked goods nearly knocked him over—brown sugar, cinnamon, citrus peel.

He had been warned, though, so he grinned as he buckled in. "Did you bake enough for an entire village?"

Edison waved a hand toward the back seat, where trays and wicker baskets balanced precariously. "Only a small hamlet. I made labels and have our route all mapped out for maximum efficiency. Maybe. I think."

Their first stop was the seniors' home, where Edison breezed forward with a broad tray wrapped in cellophane and bows. Kevin hurried ahead to hold the door. More than a couple women paused their bingo game to swoon over the treat display.

"Edison, darling," a woman in a bright purple sweater shook a finger at him from her wheelchair. "You'll be the reason my hips don't fit in my chair by next year."

"You'll dance it off," Edison said, grinning. "New Year's Eve. Save a dance for me."

The next stops blurred together as they fell into a rhythm. Since the community hall had burned down that fall, a large number of Heart Falls organizations were meeting in new temporary locations. The Boys' and Girls' Club volunteers had gathered at Rough Cut Pub, a roped-off section to one side of the dance floor full of people wrapping gifts. One of the volunteers looked ready to burst into tears over the cookie bags Edison had made to add to each gift.

At the Christmas hamper organizer's home, Edison left a huge box of non-perishable items along with a fruitcake and a hug for the coordinator herself.

Kevin mostly held baskets and opened doors and watched Edison move like sunlight through each space. Sparkling, easy, completely himself. The man's joy stirred something fierce in Kevin's chest.

"I love how you seem to know everyone in town," Kevin shared as Edison manoeuvered them out from a driveway with piles of snow five feet tall on either side. "I love how you know how to get everywhere, because I had no idea this pocket of town even existed."

"Since Dr. Jeremiah likes to do house calls, I've been taken to the most outrageous places as nursing backup." Edison lifted his chin to the left. "That road goes for about twenty minutes and then there are fifteen houses and a Hutterite Colony, tucked right up in the foothills."

And Edison knew them all and seemed to have gifts for half of them.

Eventually they pulled up to the familiar ranch house on the land Kevin currently called home. When he raised a brow at the other man, Edison grinned widely. "Last stop, Jinx."

Dixie the golden retriever met them at the front door, tail wagging so hard her hips swayed. Jinx followed a second later, face flushed from indoors warmth.

"I was hoping you'd stop by," she said, stepping aside and gesturing them in.

"Told you I would." Once inside, Edison thrust forward a paper bag decorated with shiny gold and silver cut outs. "Hope you like it."

Jinx hesitated. "Do I have to put this under the tree for Christmas day?"

Edison gasped. "Wait that long? Hell, no."

Right answer. The girl all but ripped the bag open, squealing as she pulled out a red bag stitched with gold ribbon, with small zippers and pockets lining the edges. "It's gorgeous."

"It's your new crochet bag. There's two yarn loops, so you can have the balls safely tucked away and still work on your projects while you're out by the fire." Edison's eyes sparkled. "Oh, and there's a secret snack pocket right here."

Jinx admired the bag a little more then hugged him tightly. "It's perfect, Edison. Thank you." She glanced between them. "Wait here. I didn't wrap your gifts yet, but I want you to have them now."

She raced off, Dixie barking excitedly at the high emotional energy pouring into the room.

Kevin slipped an arm around Edison's waist and squeezed. "Good job on the gift."

Edison tilted back his head and flashed Kevin a brilliant smile. "Thanks. I've been to enough nights here at High Water to know she needed one, but it had to fit her as well, you know?"

Indeed he did. Which was part of the problem. The gift he wanted to give Edison needed to fit—

"So..." Jinx had returned holding a soft, hand-crocheted scarf crafted with bright rainbow stripes. Cheerful and bright and Edison to a T. Even the slightly uneven stitches made it even more unique, just like him, and Kevin's throat tightened.

"I had so much fun making this," she said, holding the scarf out to Edison like an offering on her open palms. "I could see you wearing it."

Edison blinked fast, then took the scarf and carefully wrapped it around his neck. He glanced in the mirror beside the door before excitedly pressing both hands to his face. "Thank you a gazillion times." He hugged her again. "It's my new favourite."

A grinning Jinx turned to Kevin, pulling another object from behind her back. "I made you something too."

It was a grey neck warmer, sturdy and neat. Kevin tried it on and nodded his approval. "I love it. Thank you."

She offered him a sweet smile. "It matches you. Like Edison matches his."

And just like that, Kevin knew exactly what he was giving Edison for Christmas.

6

———————

The Christmas gathering was already in full swing inside the Heart Falls fire hall. Light glowed through the windows, the faint sound of music and laughter slipping through the door each time someone new entered.

Kevin lingered outside, waiting for Edison.

Not only for his arrival tonight—but in the bigger sense. In the life sense.

Everything had shifted since their wintery art gallery date. It wasn't just the kiss, or the way Edison had looked at him as if Kevin was made of magic. It was the quiet hope in his voice when he'd said he liked *being* with Kevin.

Kevin had never expected to fall in love with someone like Edison. Not because Edison wasn't everything good—he was. He was joy and sparkle and light in human form.

But Kevin, if he was honest, had figured he'd end up with someone...quieter. Someone closer to his own flavor of reserved. Except that wasn't how it had worked.

Thank God.

Because now? Now Kevin knew what it was to laugh so

142

hard he couldn't breathe while Edison narrated their next holiday deliveries like a game show host. He knew what it felt like to stand behind Edison in the chilly wind and watch him hug half the town with a goodie tray in one hand and his heart in the other. To witness the way people lit up when they saw him.

To feel lucky every time Edison slipped his arm into the crook of Kevin's elbow.

Kevin wouldn't change any of it. Not the brightness. Not the volume. Not even the glitter.

Especially not the glitter.

A crunch of boots over snow brought him out of his thoughts as Edison appeared around the side of the building, cheeks pink from the cold. A giant grin bloomed instantly as he caught sight of Kevin. He wore the same coat as last time—bright red with navy accents—and the rainbow scarf Jinx had made him.

Kevin's chest squeezed.

"I swear, you always show up looking like a freaking catalogue ad," Edison teased, fanning a mittened hand in front of his face. "All dapper and serious. You're hot enough to summon an early spring."

Kevin huffed a laugh and offered his arm. "And you look like the spirit of Christmas threw a parade and crowned you the grand marshal."

"Excellent," Edison said, looping their arms together. "I'll have you know I take my duties very seriously, so get ready for some serious Christmas good-cheering."

Together they continued around the side of the building toward the side yard where the annual snowman exhibit had been set up. Kevin had heard about it—one of the firefighters' pet projects—but seeing it in person was something else.

There were at least twenty snowmen. Some upright, some

toppled over. Some with scarves, some with little foam swords. A few lay face-first in the snow, and one had what looked like a plastic ribcage sticking out of its middle.

Kevin blinked. "Are they...zombies?"

"The theme this year is Snowpocalypse," Edison said proudly. "Alex told me all about it. The front-line soldiers are the good guys. The others are in full infected mode. It's very dramatic. High stakes."

A plastic flamingo had been impaled on a stick and planted like a flag. It's bird head was missing, replaced with a snowball with the classic carrot nose and coal eyes. Kevin gestured toward it. "And that one?"

"Casualty of war."

Kevin laughed, shaking his head. "Of course."

Edison pulled him toward the huddle of snowmen in the center, where a bench nestled between two upright posts with old fashioned signposts saying how far to the North Pole and Santa's workshop. Some joker had added one that gave the distance to West Edmonton Mall. Fairy lights framed the setup.

Across from the set up sat a tripod with a camera holder, and the cardboard sign read *Selfie Station.*

"Come on. We're doing this." Edison practically bounced. "The lighting's perfect, and I need to immortalize the scarf in all its glory."

Kevin let himself be dragged. "So, this is for documentation purposes?"

"It's for *thank you card* purposes," Edison replied sweetly. "Now sit."

They squished together on the bench, thighs brushing, breath visible in the air between them. Kevin tried not to stare, but Edison's lashes had caught snowflakes, little diamonds that clung to the dark curves. His cheeks were pink, his eyes impossibly bright, and Kevin's heart thudded painfully in his chest.

He wanted to say it right then.

Wanted to grab Edison's hand and say, *I love you. I think I might love you more every time you laugh. Every time you give someone a handmade gift, or talk to dogs like they're toddlers, or tell me I'm allowed to be quiet.*

Instead, he pressed a gloved hand to Edison's cheek, leaned in slowly, and kissed him.

The flash went off the exact second their lips met.

Edison fluttered his lashes. "We're going to look like a couple on the cover of a romance novel."

"You say that like it's a bad thing." Kevin grinned. "I'd be proud to model with you."

The answering *heart-in-eyes* was clear enough.

They took a few more photos—silly poses, serious ones, one with Kevin impulsively lifting Edison bridal-style, which nearly ended in both of them face-first in the snow.

Finally, Edison reached out and wrapped his arms tight around Kevin's waist. "I like this," he said softly.

Kevin rested his forehead against Edison's. "Me too."

A long moment passed. The kind where time slows down, where Kevin felt as if he could stay right there forever. With the snow falling and Edison wrapped around him because nothing else mattered.

But then Edison's arms tensed slightly. He leaned back with something in his eyes that looked suspiciously like nerves.

"As much fun as this is," he said, clearing his throat, "we should head in. I promised Yvette I'd taste test her new cranberry punch and pretend not to notice how much rum is in it."

Kevin nodded. "Lead the way."

They brushed snow from each other's coats and headed

toward the front doors of the fire hall. As they walked, Edison slipped his hand into Kevin's and held on tight.

Inside, warmth hit them in a rush along with the smell of turkey, chocolate, and cookies. Christmas lights ran across the ceiling in zigzag patterns. Someone had hung tinsel along the beams. A small stage had been set up at the back, with a mic and speakers. Music played softly in the background, some classic crooner version of "Let It Snow."

People were gathered in clusters all around them. Edison waved, and at least six smiling attendees waved back in the first ten seconds.

Kevin knew most of the Heart Falls residents now, at least by sight. He nodded at Brooke and Mack by the dessert table, exchanged smiles with Declan and Sydney, and spotted Ryan and Maddy setting out extra chairs.

Brad was by the buffet, arguing with Alex about whose meatballs smelled better. The two of them both wore appropriately ugly sweaters for the evening, although Alex's was decidedly brighter—his sweater glowed like an underwater aquarium lit with spotlights. It was as bright as if an entire string of Christmas lights were tangled around his torso.

Brad's sweater glistened in the lights, covered with way more glitter than was probably safe near an open buffet.

Edison leaned in. "Want to take bets on when the sweater competition starts?"

"Hopefully before we go blind from the flashing lights?"

"He's committed," Edison said solemnly. "You have to respect the hustle."

They were almost to the coat rack when Kevin stopped. His surprise was ready. Carefully chosen. Maybe even perfect.

But he didn't want to give it to Edison in the middle of the coat line.

Edison, still holding his hand, glanced back with a questioning smile. "You okay?"

Kevin squeezed once, grounding himself in the feeling of Edison's glove against his own. "I'm great."

The best he'd been in years. Better than great.

Because somewhere between the first delivery on Thursday and the moment they stood here now, hand in hand beneath blinking Christmas lights and surrounded by people who made them feel like family, Kevin had stopped worrying about whether Edison was too bright, too much, too dazzling for someone like him.

He'd realized that Edison was exactly what he wanted. Exactly what he needed.

And Kevin would do whatever it took to make sure Edison knew it. Even if it meant fully embracing his rainbow side— with glitter on his scarf and love in his actions.

7

———

When they'd stepped through the doors of the firehall Edison swore his heart tried to somersault its way out of his chest. All the Christmasy scents were there, and the warm air, and the noise too—laughter and chatter bouncing off every wall.

But he barely noticed any of it. He was too focused on not hyperventilating.

This was it. Tonight, he was going to tell Kevin how he felt. No hedging. No coy teasing. Just say it.

Or at least, sweater it.

Even as they moved into the chaos, he couldn't stop from glancing over at Kevin. At the little furrow between his brows as if he wasn't quite sure where to go next and he didn't want to make a mistake that would ruin the evening for anyone.

Edison's heart clenched. Kevin was perfect. All tall and thoughtful and solid, like a lamppost yet willing to bend when it was important.

Kevin's gaze met his, and his face lit up in that way that always made Edison want to sing and cry at the same time.

Okay. Now. Just do it.

No reason to wait. Edison squared his shoulders, ready to whip off his jacket as if he was presenting an award-winning science fair project titled "One Very Love-Struck Sweater."

Before he could undo a single button, a streak of motion zipped toward him.

"Mr. W" a voice squealed. He barely had time to blink before a small hand grabbed his own and tugged him off toward the far side of the hall. "Come see the marshmallow toss!"

He glanced back at Kevin, apologetic for leaving him in the lurch. Kevin only chuckled and gave him a half-salute, eyes soft with affection.

So Edison went. Of course he went. He crouched and cheered and got hit in the face by rogue marshmallows and laughed until his cheeks hurt.

It was twenty minutes later when he spotted Kevin standing beside the punch table, looking adorably uncertain about what to do with his hands. He hadn't taken off his coat either, Edison noticed with a flutter of nerves. Maybe he was waiting. Maybe he'd known Edison would need a minute to build up to this.

Edison crossed the room, his jacket still firmly in place even though it was getting very warm in the hall. "Hey, sorry. I got abducted by the sugar-gremlins."

Kevin smiled, handing him a cup. "You were a hit."

"Don't think my charm saved me. I had to bribe them with candy canes so they would let me go." He sipped the punch. Cranberry and ginger. Good, but only because it wet his suddenly dry mouth enough he could—*should*—be ready to do the next thing. "I was just about to...uh..."

Before he could continue, a clang echoed from near the kitchen, followed by a booming voice. "Change of plans! Gaudy sweater contest is before dinner, folks. Apparently, someone forgot to turn on the second oven and the sweet potatoes are not yet toasted."

Laughter rang out, and Edison blinked at Kevin. This was it. No more delays.

"I have something to show you," he said, voice shaky but determined.

Kevin turned, gaze sharp and curious. "Yeah?"

Edison nodded then reached for the zipper of his coat.

And once again, a chorus of children arrived like a confetti cannon of chaos.

"Mr. W, help me with my lights!"

"Can you untangle my battery pack?"

"Mine's blinking weird!"

He met Kevin's gaze across the swarm, helpless. Kevin just grinned and rolled up his sleeves.

They dove into the kid chaos together.

Eventually, the last blinking elf was operational, the tinsel had been secured, and Brad Ford raised his voice above the gathered ruckus. "Time for everyone to line up for the gaudy sweater parade. Strut your stuff past this year's judges now, please."

Edison found Kevin's hand in the fray and gave it a squeeze, tugging him toward a quieter corner behind the raffle table. "Okay," he said, heart thudding. "Now. For real this time."

Kevin tilted his head, clearly trying to read him. "What's going on?"

Edison cleared his throat, nerves doing jumping jacks. "I made my sweater in honour of you."

Kevin's brow rose slightly, lips twitching at the corners. "Oh?"

"It's not my usual," Edison said quickly. "I mean, it's shiny, yes, but toned down. Grown-up. A little more...you." His fingers fumbled with the zipper, but he forced it down. "I just—I wanted you to know I see you. And that I'm not afraid to meet you partway."

He tugged off his coat.

Beneath it, his sweater was slate grey with thick, knobby yarn pom-poms, like the ones that usually sat on top of a toque. They were arranged in a lopsided geometric pattern. Silver threads ran through the fabric in subtle waves, catching the light when he moved. It was stylish, quirky, and—Edison hoped—heartfelt. It was, in short, not his usual bold-and-bedazzled look, but still him. Just...adapted.

"It's supposed to be gaudy," he said with a nervous laugh. "So I couldn't go *too* understated. But I thought—maybe—it was somewhere in between the gaudy that I like and something *you'd* like."

Kevin's eyes softened, and his lips parted as if he was about to say something—when suddenly his entire face lit up like a sunrise.

"What?" Edison asked, bewildered.

Kevin's hands moved to the zipper of his own coat. "Well, funny thing."

He opened his jacket.

Edison's jaw dropped.

Because underneath Kevin's sedate black outerwear was the most gloriously awful sweater Edison had ever seen—

Bright neon green and sunflower yellow with patches of electric pink, clashing stripes across the arms, and smack dab in the middle of the chest, hand-stitched in pink yarn with a slightly crooked heart around it, was one word:

Edison.

Kevin said nothing. He didn't have to.

Edison's heart exploded.

"Oh my God," Edison breathed, tears springing to his eyes. "*Kev...*"

Kevin's ears were red, and his smile a little shy. "I thought maybe sometimes styles should change."

"You—" Edison's voice cracked. "You absolutely glorious sap."

Beyond them, the party continued. Kids laughed, adults shouted and cheered as each new gaudy sweater in the lineup hit the spotlight and the participants took a spin.

Edison barely heard any of it.

He stepped in close, eyes fixed on Kevin's sweater, then slowly looked up to meet his gaze. "That is the most ridiculous and romantic thing I've ever seen."

Kevin shrugged lightly, but his hand reached out, warm against Edison's lower back. "Seems fair. You made yours for me. I made mine for you."

Edison didn't care that half the town was in the room and might glance their direction at any moment. He reached up, cupped Kevin's face between both hands, and kissed him.

It wasn't the kind of kiss they usually shared—not the passionate ones where they were so hot for each other they couldn't think. Not the ones Edison usually gave that were shy and careful and full of possibility.

This one was certain.

Kevin kissed him back just as firmly, his arms enfolding Edison, sweater to sweater, warm through all the layers. They stood there in the chaos of the firehall, in their equally ridiculous sweaters, wrapped up in each other like some kind of makeshift holiday miracle.

When they finally pulled apart, Edison rested his forehead against Kevin's.

"I love you," he whispered, soft but true.

Kevin blinked once then grinned. "You sure?"

"Absolutely."

Kevin's arms tightened around him. "Love you, too, sunshine."

That was it. The moment. The whole thing. There wasn't a string quartet or a snow machine or a perfectly timed camera flash—though Edison was pretty sure someone in the room had snapped a photo.

It didn't matter.

This—this feeling of being wrapped in affection and safety and light—it was everything.

They stood there for another few seconds, swaying slightly as if there were music only they could hear.

Then someone near the front called, "Last call for any sweaters we haven't seen! Time to strut your gaudy stuff!"

Kevin pulled back with one final kiss to Edison's temple. "Ready?"

Edison beamed. "Oh, baby. I was born ready."

They paraded up together, hand in hand. The crowd whooped then cheered, and Edison wasn't sure his heart could hold another single teaspoon of joy. There were flashing lights and cheesy holiday music. Kevin's name was chanted by a group of teenagers lead by Jinx who were clearly thrilled to see him looking like a walking Crayola box.

Edison's heart filled to overflowing.

As the evening rolled on, Edison caught Kevin looking at him from across the room. Just looking. That steady gaze, warm and full and so achingly sure.

Edison mouthed, "You okay?"

Kevin nodded. Then, clear as day, mouthed back, "Home?"

Lordy, that was never going to get old. He crossed the room and laced their fingers together again.

Home wasn't a place.

It was a man in a sweater that said **_Edison_** in neon pink yarn.

It was a quilt on a bed that never felt empty anymore.

It was two sets of footprints in the snow—and the knowledge that going forward, Edison wasn't walking alone. Or prancing, or dancing, or whatever his heart desired.

He had Kevin, who loved him just the way he was.

One more story (starting on the next page!) will conclude our current adventures in Heart Falls series.

If you need more cowboys from me with this same sense of found family and belonging, you can go back to where it all began.

Rocky Mountain Heat is the first book in the completed Six Pack Ranch series, and there's a lot of cowboys to get to know and love, and lots of strong, determined and happy women to spend time with.

UGLY SWEATER REDUX

It's time for the annual firefighter's Christmas party, and this year the ugly sweater contest is front and center in everyone's minds.

Well, maybe not the *only* thing on their minds....

Featuring: All the firehall crew: Brad & Hanna Ford and family, Mack & Brooke and family, Ashton & Sonora Stewart, Yvette Wright & Alex Thorne, Ryan & Madison (Maddy) Zhao and family.

Timeline: This scene is set in December after the conclusion of **A Cowboy's Claim** and during the final pages of *Gifts of the Heart*.

1

Brad Ford had glitter in his beard.

He didn't know how it'd gotten there. Probably sometime between two-year-old Ethan shaking an entire vial of gold sparkles on his sweater and four year-old Drew grabbing a glue stick and smearing it directly across Brad's left sleeve.

He twisted his head to see if the shimmer that had flashed him from the kitchen window was real.

Yup. Gold and silver danced as he scratched his jaw.

He gave his wife, Hanna, a mock glare across the kitchen island as he rumbled, "This was your idea."

Hanna, completely unfazed, looked up from her own Christmas sweater-in-progress and grinned. "You said you wanted a low-key holiday evening at home."

"I meant watching *Die Hard* after the kids went to bed." Which was bullshit, and they both knew it, but his nonsense brought a flash of a smile to her face, which was a total win.

"Brad." Her tone was pure love with that hint of amusement that always got to him, "We don't do low-key around here anymore."

He huffed. But he couldn't argue.

Not when fourteen-year-old Crissy—*a teenager! When had that happened?*—was at the far end of the table helping her little brother Drew stick felt snowmen onto his sweater. The little tyke's usual wildcat energy was so focused at the moment by the importance of the task, the tip of his tongue stuck out as he carefully positioned each cutout.

Not when next to them, Ethan was covered in green puff paint and delighted about it.

And especially not when Hanna had pulled an old flannel shirt of his over her petite frame, her face lit with joy. The sight brought back many other priceless memories of her from the past years wearing his shirt and nothing else...

Fuck.

Brad loved it. All of it. Having a wife and a family. He loved the gang he worked with down at the fire hall, competitive as they were together. Hell, tonight he even loved the glitter.

He just needed a minute to grumble about it first.

"Got any extra reindeer for me?" he asked his daughter.

Crissy tossed him a pile of felt cutouts, watching with curiosity for a moment. "You're putting them on the back?"

Brad gave her a long, solemn look as he deliberately flipped the cutout to hide the comical face Hanna had sketched. Instead, he quickly redrew the antlers and legs to make the beast pop up in reverse. "No one expects reindeer *butt* on the back of my sweater. That's why I'll win."

Crissy rolled her eyes, but she snickered. "You need a bunch of fluffy tails then, Dad."

"On it." Hanna tucked a strand of hair behind Wher ear, fingers brushing his as she passed him a thread that held a vivid white pom-pom. "You're taking this very seriously."

"It's a contest," he offered, deadpan.

"It's a community gathering with a potluck and too many people shoved into the fire hall common area."

"Mack will be there, plus Ryan, Alec, and Ashton. And their wives. Stakes couldn't be higher when Madison Zhao and ugly sweaters are involved."

Hanna's amusement danced on the air, and Brad's heart did that thing it always did when she laughed—that little flip that made him feel twenty and stupid and lucky all at once. He cleared his throat and pretended to focus on positioning the reindeer's poofy tail correctly.

"*Gitter*," Ethan declared, shaking another container with wild enthusiasm before anyone could stop him.

Brad was too late to shield his sweater but managed to scoop Ethan to a safe spot on the floor before his arm swung toward the counter where dinner was cooling. "Kiddo—maybe not in the lasagna."

With a laugh, his youngest son climbed back onto the chair next to Brad. Ethan stared down at the sweater with delight. A mound of glitter clung to the place where Brad had put glue to help hold his feeble sewing attempts in place.

Ethan clapped his hands and shouted. "Sparky!"

Which meant that was the reindeer's name forevermore.

Thirty minutes later, all the sweaters neared completion, and little fingers were ready to head to the bathroom to wash up for dinner. Hanna leaned into Brad's side, resting her head on his arm. "You did great, Sparky's dad."

He kissed the top of her head then glanced toward the window.

Outside, snow fell in slow, lazy flakes, dusting the long driveway up to the ranch house. Somewhere down in town, the hall was being strung with lights, and he could already picture the welcome chaos of the annual firefighter's party. His best friend Mack's quiet steadiness, Ryan's unending patience,

Alex's sly jokes that were now one hundred percent teasing with a positive purpose.

Ashton Stewart, their representative from the older section of the community, wearing a twinkle in his eyes far more often than years before. Married life suited him.

Not to mention all the other volunteers who'd put in tons of time and energy over the past year and were ready for a chance to celebrate each other and Heart Falls. Seemed to Brad there was always something extra going on in the corners of those parties. Quiet confessions. Big surprises.

All the kids high on candy canes and laughter.

That was what they had to look forward to in a few days.

Tonight? Tonight, up here at home, it was just his family with laughter and glitter and an unexpected reindeer butt.

Brad wouldn't trade it for the world.

2

———

$\mathcal{S}$he would always have sweet memories of this time of year, Yvette Wright decided. So many good things had occurred in her life during December, a lot of them focused on the man currently pretending not to watch her.

The amused expression Alex was trying to hide was the only reason she wasn't actively threatening him.

She opened another cupboard and glanced inside. Just the dishes that were supposed to be there.

Where was it?

Yvette stood in the middle of the room and did a slow pivot. Not in the kitchen, not in the living room. Nothing new had arrived in their cabin over the past week, other than the key. Which meant *somewhere* a lock waited for her to open.

She twirled the necklace around her finger, the small gold key at the end of it whirling with a low, whistling sound.

"I hear the ugly sweater contest is shaping up to be a doozy this year." Alex said. "Mack warned me that his family's theme is going to wow the judges."

His attempt at distraction failed miserably. She kept

looking around even as she answered. "They're going as Sesame Street characters," Yvette informed him even as she poked into another drawer.

Alex blinked in surprise. "Um. Really?"

"Gaudy ones to fit the master theme of the event, but yeah. I helped Brooke source a can to place over his sweater so they could turn little Landon into Oscar the Grouch."

A loud snort echoed instantly as a wide smile bloomed. "Please tell me you suggested that a garbage can should be Mack's costume."

Too funny. Yvette turned to fully face Alex and offered her best straight face. "Well..."

His eyes widened. "You did? You *did*."

It was her turn to snicker. "A full-sized one was right there by the door," she explained, giving up on the key for a minute because this was more important. She slid onto Alex's lap, draping her arms around his neck. "They got a good laugh out of it, but they decided you and the other guys would show no mercy if Mack went that route."

"He knows us too well," Alex complained. "Still, that's an awesome theme. Too bad we're going to beat them."

She met his gaze straight on. "I agree our gaudy aquarium sweaters are the best. More on the awesomeness of us later, though, Alex. *Darling...*"

He raised a brow, hands landing firmly on her waist as he nestled her closer. "Sweetheart?"

Inch by inch, she leaned in until their lips nearly touched. "You have a present for me."

"I always have a present for you," he agreed. Mischief sparkled in his eyes.

He was such a brat. "Are you really going to make me ask?"

He nodded slowly. "Definitely. That's the perfect way to phrase it."

Confusion slipped in as Yvette considered his words. "*Ummm...*" She straightened slightly. "What?"

His lips were still curled, but his smile was softer now. Gentle, as if waiting instead of preparing for her to get excited. "*What*, what?"

She considered. Nope. Somewhere in the middle of the conversation she'd totally lost any kind of control or focus. Straight to the point, then.

Yvette leaned back and dangled the chain between them. The small key twisted slowly on the end of the long silver cord. "This belongs to something."

He nodded.

"Because as a person who is very experienced in dealing with keys, I know they're not much use without being connected to something." Yvette drifted a finger down the side of Alex's face. "And as a proof of my extensive knowledge, I present the past three years of wonderful fun and caring that you have shown by constantly providing me with new moments of anticipation in keeping with the theme of my original Christmas present."

Alex caught her fingers in his and brought them up to his lips. He pressed a kiss to them then kept holding on. "It has been three years, hasn't it?"

"Three amazing years," Yvette told him. "I've loved spending them with you. I love *you*."

He tipped his head slowly. "I feel the same, but there is one teeny, tiny thing that would make me even happier. And considering it *has* been three years, I think it's time..."

Yvette fell silent again, but this time she had more clues. She glanced down at the key draped over their linked hands.

Oh. Oh boy. He'd always said that the next step in their relationship was up to her.

Maybe this time the key wasn't a physical object that went with a physical lock.

She swallowed hard, but warmth bloomed in her chest. Was she ready?

She was. She met his gaze straight on. "Is this the key to your heart?"

He answered instantly. "Damn straight."

Yvette took a deep breath. "What do I need to do to open it?"

"Only if you're ready, but it is something I'd really like." Alex let go of her hand, lean back slightly, but when she would've wiggled off his lap, he held her in place. "Stay."

When he reached for the top buttons of his shirt, she snickered. "Is this going to be another one of these *strip each other naked* situations?"

"Eventually, I hope so, but not this instant. Trust me, sweetheart."

She watched with amusement as he undid a few more buttons then pulled back the sides of his flannel shirt.

Amusement rushed in. "Alex Thorne. You have a ring taped to the middle of your chest."

"Kind of looks that way, doesn't it?" Alex snorted. "Although, please, dear God, do not grab hold and pull. I set this up a while ago, and since you didn't arrive until later than expected, I have a sneaky suspicion that the tape has turned to superglue. You'll rip off a bunch of chest hair with it, and as excited as I am to give you a ring, I don't want that to happen."

Which meant she was laughing as she attempted to delicately peel the ring free.

"Ouch." He covered her fingers with his, trying to help. "Slow down. Wait, hang on a second..."

Alex's continuing monologue included some choice swear words as they both tried to loosen what had become a firmly matted piece of tape. The entire situation turned into something halfway perfectly romantic and a perfect farce.

Whatever else it was, the messed up, wild situation was perfectly *them*.

In the end they had to resort to a wet, warm facecloth, because Yvette refused to allow Alex to get into the shower to loosen the glue for fear that her ring would fall and go down the drain.

Eventually, when they met back at the table, both of them grinning far too hard, Alex took her hand in his and firmly slid the ring into position. "Thank you for being mine."

"I'm glad to be doing the next thing with you," Yvette said softly. "It *is* time, because you really are the one who holds the key to my heart as well."

Alex wrapped his hand around the back of her neck and pulled her in, pressing their bodies close as his lips covered hers and they sealed their engagement with a kiss.

3

———————

Brooke knew she was always welcome to stop in at the fire hall. She also knew what to do if the alarms went off and how to get out of the way as quickly as possible, which meant when the desire to stop in and see Mack hit, she had zero hesitation about caving in to the need.

It was one of the moments when Mack needed to know the news. Not in a few hours when he got off shift, but now.

She pulled eighteen-month-old Landon from his car seat into her arms. "Time to go see Daddy," she informed him.

"Twucks," he exclaimed excitedly, hanging onto her neck with one arm in a death grip. The other hand stayed free and he swung it in the air and made a loud siren sound.

She laughed. "Yes, the fire trucks are here, and sometimes the lights and sirens go off. But hopefully not right now."

She made her way up the stairs, stopping to slip off Landon's winter boots and coat before she sent him off with a pat on the bum. "Go find your daddy," she encouraged.

"Landon."

"Hey, little buddy. Are you ready for Santa to come?"

"It's the mini fire chief. Hi, bud."

Behind her, the volunteers on duty gave Landon high fives as he wobbled rapidly around the room, peering up at familiar faces, looking for his father.

Brooke hung her coat on an open wall hook then offered a wave to all as she walked farther into the common area where they'd be holding the annual gathering in just a few days.

Ashton sat at one of the tables, Landon now firmly ensconced on his lap. She made her way over and settled next to them. "Surprised to see you here. I heard a major shopping trip to Calgary was happening today."

"I'm grateful to admit I don't have the energy to keep up with the ladies anymore." Ashton offered a wink. "Or at least that's the story I'm going with."

"You're terrible," Brooke told him. "I bet you and Sonora already have all of your Christmas shopping done, don't you?"

He raised a brow. "Of course. We wrapped the last present sometime in September, but that doesn't stop Sonora. She enjoys running around with her daughter and granddaughters, doing last minute extras, far too much for me to deny her the pleasure."

"You're a good man, Ashton Stewart."

"I try to be," he offered with a grin. He leaned down to check what Landon had to say as the little boy impatiently patted the table. "What's up, kiddo?"

Brooke was slightly horrified when Landon wiggled and then used Ashton like a playground toy, climbing until he could press his little hands to either side of Ashton's face.

"Play peekaboo," Landon demanded.

Ashton laughed. "This is what I get for creating a monster. You got it, Landon." He glanced at Brooke. "Mack is in the back. Said he had a little bit of paperwork to get caught up on.

You go ahead and interrupt him, and I'll take care of our littlest firefighter."

"Thanks, Ashton." Brooke tapped Landon on the nose. "You be good for Mr. Stewart."

"He'll be just fine. Go," Ashton insisted.

Brooke paced slowly across the floor, smiling at the other volunteers who were relaxing at another table, a deck of cards in front of them.

She opened the door into the back quiet space. A couple of small bedrooms lined the side walls, and in the middle, comfy couches were arranged where anyone who needed an actual rest while on duty could slip away.

A happy memory floated in. It had been a long time since Mack had actually lived in one of those rooms.

Now they had a cozy home about a ten minute walk away from both the fire hall and the mechanic shop where Brooke continued to put in hours. Her father took care of Landon when she worked—and part-time retirement looked good on him.

Yeah, she and Mack had friends and family around them, supporting them all the way. Brooke placed a hand on the office doorknob and opened it slowly, thinking of all the blessings in their world.

Mack glanced up instantly, happy surprise on his face as he rose to his feet and stepped toward her. "Didn't expect to see you. Everything okay?"

"Everything's great," she assured him. "Landon is in the common room, large and in charge as usual."

"We're raising a miniature dictator, you know," but he smiled as he said it.

"He's got your stubbornness, that's for sure." Brooke's lips twitched with amusement. "He's got my skill with tools, though. Turned my back for a minute and he somehow took the child safety lock off one of the lower kitchen cupboards. Luckily he got distracted by the drawer next to it. The kid emptied the entire Tupperware drawer in under two minutes."

"Damn."

"Oh, that's not the interesting part. This is." She held out her phone to show off a photo she'd taken of the event. "See? He's got my skills."

Mack wrapped his hand around hers to pull the phone closer then laughed out loud at the sight of all the Tupperware stacked in tall towers. "Did he stack them according to size?"

"Yes. We've got either a mechanic or engineer in the making."

Her husband hummed in agreement. His expression went a little more serious. "What about the other thing that's in the making? How are you feeling?"

"That's why I'm here," Brooke said. She caught hold of his hand again as she twisted until her back was against his front. She laid his hand over the small bump of her belly. "Wait for it."

He went so still he had to be holding his breath.

Brooke closed her eyes and breathed slowly for both of them. For all *three* of them, she corrected herself, and another rush of happiness flooded in as she thought about this blessing as well.

Under his hand, the baby fluttered. The smallest of movements, but with this being baby number two, Brooke knew what the sensation meant.

"They just started this morning," Brooke told him, leaning her cheek against his. "Everything's going well. Almost halfway through the pregnancy, and I'm so happy."

Mack kissed her cheek. Fingers spreading wide as he continue to carefully cradle her belly. He wrapped his other arm around her torso and hugged her tightly. "I'm glad you came to tell me."

"She's going to have you wrapped around her little finger." Brooke twisted in his arms and smiled up into his eyes. "I figured we may as well start right now."

"Still insisting this one's a girl? Even though we have no proof?"

Brooke considered. "Yep. She's a girl. I just—know."

Mack grinned. "I hope you're right, but if you're not, I'm still going to be good. Now, you said Landon was out there somewhere?"

"Tormenting Ashton."

"I approve of that." Mack grabbed her fingers. He guided her from the office and back toward the main area. "Let me give the kiddo a hug. And tonight we'll put the finishing touches on our ugly sweaters, yes?"

She followed him into the wide open space, arriving just in time to hear Landon squealing with happiness as Ashton's deep laugh boomed on the air.

"Only two more days until the party. We better make sure we're ready," Brooke agreed.

"To win," Mack said with a gloating tone.

"To win," she agreed, but the outcome of the contest wasn't anything she was worried about.

As far as Brooke was concerned, she'd already won.

4

———

They needed to go in early to finish setting up for the party. That's what Ryan had told her. His parents, who were temporarily living with the family once again, would bring the kids by just before the event started.

Her husband had a second agenda beyond party prep.

Madison Zhao swallowed the moan that wanted to escape, leaning her hips farther back into Ryan as the heated water sluiced down both their naked bodies. "You're killing me," she whispered.

A low, dirty laugh escaped him, and whatever magic he was doing with his fingers between her legs increased in tempo. "No, killing us is having my parents living with us, using our bedroom, and us sleeping on an air mattress in the living room where we have no privacy."

Tension ratchetted upward rapidly as Maddy let her head fall back on his shoulder. One minute after arriving in an empty yet completely decorated and prepped fire hall, Ryan had pulled her into one of the private rooms at the back, stripped them both naked, and tugged her into the shower with him.

Not that she was complaining. "Stop talking and fuck me already."

"Such language," he teased. "No wonder our three-year-old caused a ruckus in the grocery store the other day when Justin started singing a song about shit."

"Wasn't my fault," Maddy protested. "I'll explain...*later.* Oh, please."

"Much later," Ryan agreed.

He spun her, pressed her back to the wall, then dropped to his knees. A moment later Maddy teetered on one leg, the other draped over his broad shoulder as Ryan covered her sex with his mouth and went to town.

She clutched his head for balance then stared down to take in every second. His blue black-hair stuck up in messy tufts as water ran in small rivulets over her belly and onto him. Pleasure spiraled upward as he continued to work, and she caught her lip between her teeth and hummed quietly.

A soft laugh escaped him, and all of it slipped over her in a moment of near perfection. Ryan, giving as usual, such a strong link between them that when he stood and slipped his cock deep, it was the final coming home she needed.

"*Ryan.*" His name rushed out as a wave started in her core and spread.

He stared into her eyes, lips curled in a smile as he rocked deep, over and over, the motion dragging out her orgasm until he too gave in. His eyes closed briefly then reopened, complete connection and love in their depths.

They washed up slowly afterward, hands continuing to caress and touch, all the way until they were dressed again and ready to rejoin the rest of the world.

"Thanks for the secret moment to ourselves," Maddy whispered before Ryan opened the door.

"We deserved it," Ryan offered, kissing her one final time before pushing open the door. "And now you can tell me about the shit song."

Which meant she was laughing as they joined the others now gathered in the common room. The scent of turkey and ham and sweet pumpkin spice carried on the air as they made their way to the side of the room where games for the kids would be run.

"Your dad found a comedian who did a whole routine about how funny the English language is about the word shit. Stuff like...don't touch my shit because it's important, yet other people's shit is annoying..."

"Oh no," Ryan muttered.

"It was a funny routine," Maddy informed him primly. "Only Dad played it for me, then your mom, then another half dozen times over the phone for friends. None of us realized Justin was awake from his nap and listening the whole time."

"Little mastermind," Ryan said proudly.

"Wait until I tell you about our fifteen-month-old. Mikayla said 'duck' to your mom." Maddy snickered. "I'm positive she wasn't talking about the floaty toy."

Ryan's lips twitched.

Maddy patted Ryan's chest, admiring how the traditional gaudy sweater stretched across his body.

His phone went off, and he checked it quickly. "Mom and Dad are here with the kids." He smiled at her. "Having a nearly sixteen-year-old who can drive is a glorious thing, when I'm not scared to death about Talia behind the wheel."

"She's an excellent driver," Maddy assured him. "Let's go grab them. We can make a grand entrance as a gaudily dressed family."

At the base of the stairs, Ryan paused then let out a contented sigh as Maddy stepped beside him. She spotted what had his attention.

Ryan's parents stood a few feet inside the main doors, right beside the shiny, polished trucks. They chatted enthusiastically with Ashton and Sonora Stewart, the lot of them all wearing sweaters in a wild assortment of bright colours.

Justin held onto his grandpa's hand, his dark hair slicked neatly into place. Talia waited beside them, adjusting the bright yellow barrette in Mikayla's pale reddish curls.

"Maddy, can I get your help?" The call came from the room above them.

"Of course. One minute," she called back.

Ryan gave her a squeeze. "You go. I'll get the family. We'll meet when it's time..."

"We'll meet a dozen times before then," Maddy promised before hurrying away.

The next hour was chaos at its finest. The common room slowly filled, and filled some more, until Maddy was a little concerned they were on the verge of breaking some maximum occupancy regulations. And wouldn't that be annoying considering the fire hall was the one to put the regs in place in town.

"Looking good, Mad." Brooke breezed past, the cookie monster on her sweater holding a three dimensional jar to hold the cookies. The bulge of her growing baby belly formed the swell of the jar, and Maddy approved.

"You, too," Maddy offered sincerely. She spotted potential trouble on the horizon, though. "Favour to ask. Can you guys go make sure the marshmallow toss has more tossing of the material than eating of them? We're going to run out of supplies at this rate."

"On it," Brooke promised. "Come on, guys. We have marshmallows to save."

Mack winked at Maddy. His sweater looked like a tinsel covered brick wall, and the small plastic garbage can he'd rigged with a sling rested at hip level. Little Landon sat in the can, his ruffled hair poking up every direction. The shoulders of a very fluffy and ragged green sweater just visible as the two of them twisted to follow Brooke.

Very Oscar the Grouch vibes.

"This evening gets stranger and stranger every year, and I love it," Yvette said as she paused beside Maddy.

Maddy took a good look at her. A glowing pale blue nimbus surrounded her friend as the fish and other sea creatures on Yvette's sweater swam back and forth in slow circles.

"How are you doing that?" Maddy demanded. She leaned in closer. "Are those LEDs?"

"Fiber optics and teeny processors, and that's where I can't answer any more details because Alex got this together with Petra from High Water, and the tech talk they tossed at each other while figuring out how to make it work was above my paygrade."

"It's sick."

"Thanks." Yvette glanced around the room and hummed happily. "Good turn out."

"Lots of new volunteers this year," Maddy pointed out. "With the community hall burning down this fall, there was a rush of community spirit. We have more helpers than we need at times."

"A good problem to have."

A clang echoed from near the kitchen, followed by a familiar voice.

Brad Ford called out loudly enough for everyone to hear. "Change of plans! Gaudy sweater contest is before dinner, folks. Apparently, someone forgot to turn on the second oven and the sweet potatoes are not yet toasted."

Oops. Maddy glanced around to see where she was needed then hurried to help get the spotlight lined up properly.

Music played, and laughter rang out. In singles or groups, everyone took their turn stepping into the spotlight and twisting so that everyone could admire their sweaters. As the fourth official year for the sweater contest, everyone had fully embraced the event.

At one point something bright flashed from a corner of the room that didn't seem to have anything to do with the contest, but Madison was more focused on the here and now. On her friends and family all coming together once again to celebrate being community. Being important to each other and being there for each other.

One ugly sweater at a time.

"Ready for our turn?" Ryan slipped his hand into hers. He held Mikayla in his other arm. This year, their family sweaters were a starburst of red and green checkerboard.

Their daughter reached out. "Mama."

"Gotcha, baby girl." Maddy cuddled her in close then settled her on a hip just as Justin grabbed hold of a pant leg.

Talia picked up her brother then stood happily beside her father. "Ready, Mom?"

Maddy smiled at Talia then met Ryan's eyes. "It's showtime. Come on, family."

They stepped into the spotlight together.

ABOUT THE AUTHOR

New York Times and *USA Today* bestselling author Vivian Arend loves to share the products of her over-active imagination with her readers. She writes contemporary, western, and light-hearted paranormal romances. The stories are humorous yet emotional, usually with a large cast of family or friends, and a guaranteed happily-ever-after. Vivian lives in British Columbia, Canada, with her husband of many years—her inspiration for every hero and a willing companion for all sorts of adventures.

www.vivianarend.com